W9-BCO-831

. . . but at what cost?

In Search of Andy

MARILYN KAYE

BANTAM BOOKS
NEW YORK • TORONTO • LONDON • SYDNEY • AUCKLAND

RL 5.5, 008–012
IN SEARCH OF ANDY
A Bantam Skylark Book / June 2000

ISBN 0-553-48713-2

Visit us on the Web! www.randomhouse.com/kids

Published simultaneously in the United States and Canada

Bantam Skylark is an imprint of Random House Children's Books, a division of
Random House, Inc. SKYLARK BOOK and colophon and BANTAM BOOKS and
colophon are registered trademarks of Random House, Inc. Bantam Books, 1540
Broadway, New York, New York 10036.

PRINTED IN THE UNITED STATES OF AMERICA

OPM   10   9   8   7   6   5   4   3   2   1

For Corinne, who gave me Paris
and continues to give me joie de vivre

In Search
of Andy

one

" **G**o! Go! Go!"

Amy Candler shrieked along with the rest of the girls on her team as the relay runner carrying the baton raced toward her. The runner on the other team had just passed the baton to the last girl in their lane.

"Come on, Carrie!" Amy yelled. P.E. was almost over, and this was the final event in a series of competitions held that day. Amy's side was ahead, but the other team would be tied if it won the relay race. As the final runner on *her* team, Amy stood poised to snatch the baton as soon as Carrie came within snatching distance.

Finally the girl reached her. Amy could hear her teammates screaming, "Go, Amy!" as she took off. Without much effort, she caught up to her opponent and passed her. It looked like Amy was going to cruise to the finish line, but as soon as she caught a flash of the gym teacher's startled expression, Amy knew she was running way too fast. Faster than any normal twelve-year-old girl. Immediately she slowed down and hoped the teacher would just think her eyes had been playing tricks on her. But Amy didn't calculate her change of pace well, and now the girl from the opposing team was passing her.

Amy tried to adjust her speed so she could move ahead again, but as she attempted to figure out exactly how fast she should run, the other girl reached the finish line.

Of course, Amy's teammates didn't blame Carrie, who had slowed them down in the first place, for their loss.

"Good going, Amy," someone mumbled sarcastically, and she didn't miss the dirty looks a couple of others shot her. Amy's shoulders slumped and she ducked her head as the class straggled back to the locker room. She knew that by the time they'd showered and dressed, everyone would have forgotten that she'd been the last runner on the losing team. Still, she felt crummy.

Lately it seemed like this kind of thing was always happening to her. She'd be all set to do her best, which was always better than anyone else could achieve, when she'd hear her mother's voice, way in the back of her mind, warning her.

Don't show off, Amy. It's too dangerous. You can't let anyone see what you're capable of doing. You must not let anyone know what you are. Just be average.

She'd heard those words a zillion times, and she knew her mother was right. But it wasn't easy to be average. Just that morning, in algebra, the teacher had scrawled a problem on the board and asked for a volunteer to solve it. Amy's hand had shot up automatically—until she remembered that she'd solved the previous problem. It was too late. The teacher had seen her hand and called on her. Amy fumbled and stuttered and blurted out an answer so unbelievably wrong that the teacher was appalled and one classmate laughed out loud.

"It's so embarrassing," Amy complained to her best friend, Tasha Morgan, as they walked home from school that afternoon. "It's hard being ordinary. When I try not to be the best, I end up being the worst."

Tasha wasn't terribly sympathetic. "Am I supposed to feel sorry for you because you're not ordinary?"

"I'm not asking you to feel sorry for me!"

"Sure you are. You're complaining because you're perfect. How do you think that makes *me* feel?"

Amy was utterly bewildered. "Tasha, what are you talking about?"

"You are intellectually and physically superior to me, and you're still not happy with yourself. So that means I should feel even worse about *me*."

Amy groaned. She knew where this was coming from. "Tasha, have you been reading that stupid self-help book again?"

"It's not stupid," Tasha answered. "And don't belittle my efforts."

"Huh?"

Tasha reached into her bag and pulled out *How to Be Your Own Goddess*. Opening it, she read aloud. " 'As you move forward toward the goal of worshipping your inner self, there will be people who will mock and belittle your efforts to realize the goddess that dwells within you. Until you have reached your goal, avoid these people. Do not permit them to assert or impose their attitudes. They are not superior to you.' "

"Tasha! I've never said I was superior to you!"

"I know," Tasha acknowledged. "But you *are*. I'm an ordinary twelve-year-old girl. You're a genetically engineered clone. You're stronger than I am, you're quicker than I am, you're better than me in every possible way."

"That's not *my* fault," Amy said. "There's nothing I can do about it. It's the way I was born. If you can call getting cooked up in a laboratory being born," she added.

"It doesn't matter," Tasha said. "Whether you mean to or not, you make me feel inferior."

"Oh, that's silly."

Tasha glanced at her. "See? Now you say I'm silly for having feelings."

"Don't be stupid."

"And now you're calling me stupid," Tasha said sadly. "Amy, I don't think we should spend so much time together."

"*What?*"

"According to this book, I need to separate myself from friends who make me feel . . . well, not like a goddess."

Amy couldn't believe what she was hearing. "So you're saying we're not best friends anymore?"

"Oh, no, it's nothing like that," Tasha quickly assured her. "We just need to take a break. I need some time to gather my inner resources and acknowledge myself as the goddess that I am."

Personally, Amy thought this whole business sounded

like utter nonsense, but she held her tongue. "For how long?"

"I'm not sure. A week, maybe two."

"We're not going to speak to each other for two weeks?"

Tasha checked the instructions in her book. "We can speak," she said finally. "We just can't hang out."

"Starting when?" Amy wanted to know. They'd reached the block where they both lived.

Tasha bit her lip. "Now?" She frowned. "See, there I go again, asking your permission. I have to take positive action. We start *now*." She stuck the book back in her bag and gave Amy a quick hug. "It's all for the best. We'll be even better friends, because I'll be feeling really good about myself. See ya!" She ran off toward her house.

Amy stared after her and tried not to feel glum. She'd known Tasha for a long time; they'd been best friends forever, and she knew how Tasha could get caught up in one fad or another. She sincerely doubted this separation would last two weeks.

But she'd assumed she would be hanging out with Tasha this afternoon, and now she had nothing to do. It was so nice out today, warm and sunny, real southern California weather. She didn't feel like going into her empty house. Her mother was teaching at the university for at least another hour. Her boyfriend, Eric, Tasha's brother, was still at school, in detention. He was always getting detention, mainly for oversleeping and arriving after the bell.

Amy wondered if her next-door neighbor, Monica Jackson, was home. Monica was an artist and a jewelry maker, and sometimes she had neat, weird new stuff to show Amy. If nothing else, Monica changed her hair color almost weekly, and with her glamorous makeup and outrageous outfits, it was always fun just looking at *her*.

But when Monica came to the door, she didn't look terribly interesting. Her hair was the same baby pink it had been the last time Amy saw her, almost a month ago, only now there were dark roots growing in. Her face was devoid of its usual mask of dramatic makeup, and she wore plain jeans and a T-shirt. There wasn't a spark of glitter anywhere on her.

She gazed at Amy mournfully. "Is it nice out?" she asked vaguely.

"Very," Amy replied.

Monica opened the door and came out, blinking as if she hadn't seen the sun in a millennium. She plopped down on the steps and uttered a deep, heavy sigh.

Amy got the cue. "What's the matter, Monica?"

Other adults usually said, "Oh, nothing," or brushed

her off, but Monica wasn't like other adults. She treated Amy like an equal. "Sam and I broke up."

"I'm sorry to hear that," Amy said, trying to remember who Sam was. Monica's boyfriends came and went, and none of them stayed too long. "Did you guys have a fight?"

"In a way," Monica replied. "He says he's not ready to make a commitment." She punctuated this with another sigh. "You know, Amy, I'm the same age as your mother. I'm ready to commit. I want to settle down. How come men don't want to do that?"

"I don't know," Amy replied honestly. There had to be some who wanted to settle down. It was just that Monica chose the wrong men. Personally, Amy thought they were all losers.

"Maybe I should just give up," Monica said. "Or at least take a break. That's what I need, Amy. A vacation from men. No flirting, no dating." She got up and smiled wistfully. "You're lucky you don't have these problems yet," she murmured before going back inside.

Amy wasn't so sure this was true. Eric was usually a pretty decent boyfriend, but that didn't mean their relationship was problem-free. That very moment, he was coming down the street with one of the problems.

Amy didn't *hate* Nick Porter—he just happened to be

her least favorite of Eric's friends. Nick was a clown, the kind of guy who liked to start food fights in the cafeteria at school. And sometimes, when Eric was with him, *Eric* started acting clownish too.

She got up and went to meet them on the sidewalk. "Hi, how was detention?"

The boys exchanged grins. "Better than usual," Eric said. "Show her the box, Nick."

Nick pulled a small blue box from his backpack and opened it. Inside were two chirping crickets.

Amy rolled her eyes.

t w 2

"Paris," Amy repeated. "Paris, *France*?"

Her mother nodded happily. "It's a major international conference, and the most important people in my field will be there. One of my colleagues at the university was selected to go, but now she has the flu. So I'm going in her place! Amy, this could be wonderful for my career and my reputation."

"Paris," Amy breathed. She took French at school, and her teacher, Madame Duquesne, was always talking about Paris. She'd shown the class her slides of the city, and they'd watched movies set there. Everyone, including Amy, had agreed that Paris was the most beautiful, the most romantic-looking place in the whole world. Paris, the City of Light . . . the Eiffel Tower, the magnificent churches and palaces, the sidewalk cafés. Images from the slides danced in Amy's head.

She felt incredibly lucky. Here she was, longing to take a break from her normal life. She would have settled for a weekend at the beach in Santa Monica. Instead, she was going to Paris, France!

"When do we leave?" she asked.

Her mother looked momentarily blank. "We?" Then her eyes went soft. "Oh, honey, I'm sorry. I can't take you with me."

"Mom! Why not? You took me to that conference in Seattle last year!"

Nancy shook her head. "That's not a fair comparison, Amy. Paris is a lot farther away than Seattle. You can't miss a whole week of school." She must have seen the disappointment in Amy's face, because she really did look very sorry. "Sweetie, it wouldn't be any fun for you. I'll be totally involved with this conference, going to meetings and lectures every day. In the evenings, I'll probably have to attend a lot of official functions. There'll be no time for me to take you sightseeing, and you can't run around Paris by yourself. Besides, the trip would be way too expensive, and the university will only pay for my ticket."

Amy hung her head in silent despair. In her mind, all the lights of Paris were going out.

Nancy put an arm around her. "I'm going to ask Monica if she'll stay here with you while I'm gone. You'll like that. You always have fun with Monica." She wrapped her other arm around Amy and gave her a quick hug. "Look on the bright side, honey. This conference could mean a big promotion for me, and that means a big raise. And if I get a big raise, maybe next summer you and I can go to Paris together on a real vacation."

There were too many *mights*, *maybes*, and *ifs* for Amy. For the rest of the evening, she moped. Nancy barely noticed. She was too busy getting ready for the conference.

As Amy lay in bed that night, she knew she shouldn't make her mother feel guilty about the trip. It was a business trip, after all. It wasn't as if she wouldn't take Amy along if she could. There were just too many obstacles standing in the way.

With her thumb and forefinger, Amy rubbed the pendant that hung around her neck. It was something she always did when she felt overwhelmed by a problem she couldn't resolve easily. She didn't expect anything magical to happen when she fingered the crescent moon–shaped charm. But it always reminded her that she was special, and that meant sometimes she could come up with special solutions.

The pendant had been given to her by Dr. Jaleski. Twelve years ago, he had been the director of Project Crescent, in which Nancy Candler and other scientists had been experimenting with superior genetic material. By studying the identical clones they produced from the material, they hoped to learn how to prevent genetic disorders. At least, that was what they *thought* the goal of the experiment was. But the mysterious government organization that was funding the project had a different goal. They wanted to gain world domination through the creation of superior people, a master race.

When the project members realized this, they immediately and secretly arranged for the clones, the twelve Amys, to be distributed to adoption agencies around the world. Nancy Candler had taken Amy, Number Seven home to raise as her own daughter. Then the scientists blew up the laboratory and claimed the clones had perished in the explosion.

In the past year, certain incidents had led both Amy and her mother to believe that the organization had never been convinced that the clones were destroyed. When Amy learned of her special situation, Nancy had taken her to Dr. Jaleski so that he could explain everything to her. Soon after, Dr. Jaleski had been murdered—probably to keep him from saying more.

That was why Amy had to be very careful not to draw attention to her extraordinary skills. It was quite possible that the organization had never given up on their plans, and that they still wanted to get their hands on Amy and the other clones. The Amys' perfect DNA was the key to creating additional physically and intellectually superior human beings.

Despite the dangers, Amy certainly didn't mind being way better than average. But if she was so superior, physically and mentally, why couldn't she think of a way to overcome Nancy's objections and accompany her to Paris? Maybe she'd wake up the next morning with the answer.

She didn't. Her mind was still blank.

At breakfast, her mother made phone calls and wrote lists, searched for her passport, and checked the Weather Channel on TV for the current conditions in Paris. Amy wished she could talk with Tasha, since Tasha had a knack for coming up with creative solutions. But Tasha wouldn't be coming by to walk with her to school.

Amy left early, hoping that a solitary walk might produce brilliant ideas. If only her superior skills included a little magic, like the ability to fly or become invisible. She wondered how long a clone could survive stowed away in a piece of luggage. . . .

When the answer to her problem came, it was totally unexpected. It happened in algebra, when she remembered to keep her hand down as the teacher put the daily big problem on the board. Watching the students struggling with the elaborate equation, Amy was bored. The answer was totally clear to her, but it was obviously complicated for a person of normal intelligence.

She was barely listening as the teacher tried to help the students. "Break it down," the teacher said. "Don't let it overwhelm you. Take each component one at a time. Be logical. Instead of treating it as one big problem, break it down into a series of small problems and address each one independently." The teacher went to the board and started to write, "#1, #2, #3 . . ."

That was when a lightbulb went on in Amy's head.

What a concept! She could overcome all her mother's obstacles—and she didn't even need to use any of her special talents. There was a solution to each of her mother's objections. All she needed to do was break them down and attack each one separately. She recalled each part of her mother's explanation as to why Amy couldn't go with her to Paris.

#1. Amy couldn't miss a whole week of school.

Amy addressed that problem in third-period French class. She arrived before anyone else and went straight to Madame Duquesne.

"*Bonjour,* Amy."

"*Bonjour, Madame.*" Amy switched to English. "Madame, do you think travel is educational?"

"*Mais bien sûr*—of course!"

"Would you put that in writing?"

#2. Nancy would have no time to take Amy sightseeing, and she didn't want Amy running around Paris by herself.

Amy attacked that problem on her way home from school. She knocked on Monica's door, and when her neighbor answered, she got straight to the point.

"You know what you need, Monica? A vacation from men. You need to spend a week in a place where there are so many interesting distractions, you won't even think about guys and dates."

"Like where?"

Amy told her.

#3. The trip was too expensive.

Amy went home and got on the Internet. It wasn't too difficult to locate Web sites that offered travel bargains. In no time at all, she found an airline that was offering a two-for-one special from Los Angeles to Paris.

When Nancy came home from the university that evening, Amy was ready.

"Mom, I'm going to Paris with you."

"Oh, honey, I wish you could, but—"

Amy interrupted. "Here's a letter from my French teacher," she said, handing her mother an envelope.

The envelope contained a letter praising the benefits of travel as being more educational than a week in school, and as the best way to perfect a language. Her mother looked impressed. "This is certainly very persuasive, Amy. But—"

Amy broke in again. "I know you won't be able to spend any time with me and that I can't run around Paris by myself. Well, Monica wants to go to Paris too. She can look after me there just as easily as here."

"I suppose so. But—"

"It's too expensive. Well, Monica says she can afford to buy her own ticket, and I found an airline that's offering a two-for-one special."

There were no more *but*s. In fact, her mother appeared to be momentarily speechless.

"What do you say, Mom?"

Nancy Candler looked as if she'd been hit on the head. She was totally stunned. Finally she spoke.

"I say it looks like you're coming to Paris with me."

three

Amy didn't understand how her mother could sleep. Sitting in the same seat for ten hours wasn't exactly exciting, even though there had been two meals and three movies to entertain them. But how could anyone sleep, knowing that in—she checked the screen that reported the progress of the plane—less than one hour, they would be in Paris!

On her other side, Monica was awake, totally engrossed in a guidebook.

"What are you reading about?" Amy asked her.

"*Mona Lisa.* You know, the famous painting by Leonardo Da Vinci. It hangs in the Louvre Museum."

"Maybe we can go see it," Amy said.

"Of course we'll see it! I studied this painting and many more when I was in art school. Now I can't believe I'm actually going to see the real thing!"

"Yeah, that'll be cool."

"You know, Amy, I've been thinking. Your mother said this trip had to be educational for you. Well, how about if I give you a whole course in art history in Paris? We could spend the whole week going to museums. What do you think?"

Amy was skeptical. True, Monica was an artist, but her art was wild and weird—not the kind you saw in museums. And Amy had never been all that interested in art history. "But we can do other stuff too, right?" she asked anxiously. She thought about some of the places she'd read about in her guidebook. "I want to see the Eiffel Tower, and the gardens, and the Catacombs, and—"

"The what?"

"The Catacombs." Amy closed her eyes and quoted from the guidebook on her lap. " 'Under Paris there are miles of tunnels where bodies were buried when the cemeteries became overcrowded in the eighteenth century. Today, you can see stacks of bones and skulls along the corridors.' "

Monica shuddered. "No thanks, I prefer to stay

aboveground among the living." She went back to her own guidebook. "Some of the finest Impressionist paintings are in Paris, Amy. We're going to have a whole week of pure culture. No silly social stuff. All this glorious art will definitely keep my mind off men!" She began rattling off the names of museums. There had to be a thousand of them, and she seemed intent on exploring each one.

Amy tuned her out. She began making her own mental check marks. At the top of her list were the Catacombs. She hoped they sold postcards of the skulls. She definitely wanted to send one to Eric. That would impress him a lot more than a postcard of the *Mona Lisa*.

She wondered if Eric missed her yet. Being separated could be a good thing. Maybe he'd come to realize that a loudmouthed buddy was no substitute for an intelligent and fun girlfriend. As for Tasha, by the end of the week she should have found her inner goddess and decided she'd rather have a best friend.

Suddenly Amy realized that a flight attendant was speaking in French over the intercom. But before she could translate the words, the woman repeated them in English.

"We are beginning our descent into Paris' Charles de Gaulle Airport. Please check to make sure your seat belts are securely fastened, and that your seats and tray tables are in their upright position." She went on with some instructions about disconnecting electronic devices, but Amy had stopped listening.

"Mom, wake up! We're almost there!" She leaned across her mother and peered out the window. The French clouds didn't look any different from American clouds. She could feel her ears pop as the plane began its descent.

The landing was smooth, and the plane taxied to the terminal. From then on, everything was a blur of noise and movement. And waiting. After they'd gathered their stuff from the overhead bins, Amy waited with her mother and Monica to make their way down the aisle of the crowded plane. Then they waited in a long line for a French official to look at their passports. Next they waited for their luggage. Then they waited to go through customs. Finally they were free to leave the airport. But even outside, they had to stand in a long line for a ride into the city of Paris.

When they were at last settled in the backseat of a taxi, Amy leaned forward and spoke to the driver.

"*S'il vous plaît, nous voulons aller à rue Beaumont, numéro soixante-huit.*"

She glanced at her mother and Monica, neither of whom spoke French and who had no idea she'd just told the driver they wanted to go to 68 Beaumont Street. They both looked impressed. The taxi driver, however, was not.

"Pardon?" he asked. He put the accent on the second syllable, but the word meant the same thing in French as in English.

Amy repeated her request. This time the man turned to look at her, his face a total blank. *"Pardon?"* he asked again.

Amy told him the address a third time, making sure to speak very slowly. The man still didn't understand. Finally Nancy handed him a card with the name and address of their hotel.

"Ah, oui!" the driver said, saying the address out loud. He spoke the same words that Amy had spoken, but they sounded completely different coming from his lips. The car took off, and Amy sank back into her seat.

What had she done wrong? She was taking French at school. Just yesterday she'd read ahead in her textbook and memorized tons of words and grammar rules. She must have been pronouncing everything badly. And all the vocabulary in the world wouldn't do her any good if no one could understand a word she was saying.

Well, she wasn't going to worry about it now. Pressing her nose against the window, she got excited all over again. At first the highway looked like any highway anywhere. But when they actually arrived in the streets of Paris, she knew she wasn't in Los Angeles anymore.

Old buildings with ornate doors and windows lined the sidewalks. In front of cafés, little tables were squeezed together, and waiters in long aprons balanced trays as they darted among the customers. Even the cars on the streets weren't like the ones Amy was used to seeing in L.A. Some were so tiny she couldn't imagine how normal-size people could fit in them. And there were little shops everywhere . . . a bakery with gorgeous fancy treats in the window . . . another shop with big fat sausages dangling from the ceiling . . . Of course, all the signs over the shops were in French. At least Amy had no problem reading them.

The taxi stopped at a red light, and Monica pointed to a restaurant on the corner. "Ooh, that's so cute!" she gushed. "Look, the menu is posted outside. I bet the food is delicious. What does it say, Amy?"

Amy studied the menu written on the large slate. *Escargots . . . pieds de cochon . . . tête de veau.* "Snails, pig's feet, calf's head," she translated. "Yeah, I'll bet that's real yummy."

Monica turned green.

"Don't worry," Amy reassured her. "Look, there's a McDonald's and a Pizza Hut!"

"I did *not* come to Paris to eat a Big Mac," Monica

informed her. "I plan to be very brave and try everything. Well, maybe not the calf's head."

The taxi squealed to a halt in front of their hotel. Amy had memorized the French currency, but after her earlier embarrassment, she allowed her mother to struggle with figuring out how much money they owed the driver.

Thank goodness the man at the hotel reception desk spoke English. When Nancy told him her name, he nodded immediately.

"Yes, Madame Candler, we have been expecting you. Your room is ready." He handed her a key. "Room 203. Do you require assistance with your luggage?"

"No thank you, I can manage," Nancy murmured. "And the other room, is it ready too?"

"Pardon?"

"The second room I reserved. For my daughter and Ms. Jackson."

"I am sorry, Madame. I have nothing here about a second reservation." A telephone rang, and he answered it.

"Maybe the room has three beds," Amy suggested. "Let's go look."

But there was hardly enough space in the room to accommodate the one single bed that was there. They went back down to the lobby.

"Excuse me," Nancy said to the receptionist. "We

25

will need a second room. Or a larger room for the three of us."

The man looked stricken. "This is unfortunate, Madame. There are no more rooms available. With the biology conference, this hotel is completely full."

Now Nancy was dismayed. "Is there another hotel nearby?"

"I will see." The man got on the phone and made several calls during which he spoke rapid French. Amy tried to understand what he was saying, but he was speaking much too fast.

"I am terribly sorry, Madame," he said, hanging up the phone. "There are no vacancies in the hotels of this area. However, I have been able to locate a double room in a small hotel on the Left Bank."

Nancy wasn't happy. "But this is the Right Bank, isn't it?"

"Madame, the Left Bank is the other side of the River Seine. It is not a terribly wide river." He wrote down the address of the second hotel.

"Don't worry, Nancy," Monica said. "I'll be there with Amy. And I'm sure it's a perfectly nice place."

But Nancy insisted on going with them to check out the other hotel. Once again they got into a taxi. This time Amy didn't even try to give directions. She let her mother hand the man the paper with the address written on it.

They crossed a bridge that looked so ancient Amy wondered why it didn't collapse under the weight of all the cars going back and forth. But they made it safely to the other side, and into another area of charming old buildings and narrow streets. The driver let them out in front of one of the smaller buildings. Alongside the door was a plaque that read LA MAISON DE LA SOURIS.

Amy decided not to tell Monica or her mother that the hotel's name in English was "The House of the Mouse." She just hoped it wasn't an actual description of any particular inhabitant. Entering the lobby, she breathed a sigh of relief. It wasn't as grand as the hotel where her mother was staying, but it looked perfectly clean, and she didn't see any mice running along the walls. A plump, gray-haired woman greeted them warmly.

"Bonjour, Mesdames, Mademoiselle, bienvenue. Je m'appelle Madame Anselme. Votre chambre est prête. Venez avec moi, s'il vous plaît."

It took Amy a minute to think over the words, but she was pleased to be able to tell the others that the woman's name was Madame Anselme, that she was welcoming them, and that their room was ready. They followed her up two flights of stairs.

The room was small, but there were two beds and an adorable little balcony. Amy thanked the woman with a *"Merci beaucoup,"* and she was pleased to see that the woman appeared to understand.

Monica fell onto one of the beds. "How do you say 'I need a nap' in French?"

"No, no, you can't sleep," Nancy informed her. "That's the worst thing you can do right now."

Monica looked at her watch. "But it's midnight!"

"That's Los Angeles time," Nancy reminded her. "In Paris it's nine o'clock in the morning. If you sleep now, you'll never adjust to the time difference, and you'll have jet lag all week. What you should do is take a quick shower, change your clothes, and go out for some coffee. I'm going downstairs to arrange payment with Madame Anselme."

Amy took the first shower and changed, and as Monica went into the tiny bathroom, Amy joined her mother downstairs.

"I would be so grateful if you could keep an eye on my daughter, Amy," Nancy was telling Madame Anselme. "My friend will be staying here with her, of course, but I'm still going to worry. Do you have children?"

"Oui, Madame," the manager said, smiling.

"Then you must know how I feel. Amy is a good girl;

she won't be any trouble, but she can be very independent for a twelve-year-old."

"*Oui, Madame.*"

"I'll be calling every day to check on her. She may be out when I call, but you'll let me know if there are any problems, won't you?"

"*Oui, Madame.*"

Amy grimaced. She didn't really want to have the hotel manager bugging her the way her mother did at home. Nancy, however, seemed relieved that this motherly woman would be looking out for Amy. "Amy, be good, enjoy yourself, but listen to Monica and Madame Anselme, okay? I have to go get ready for a meeting, but I'll call you tonight." She embraced Amy and ran out the door.

Amy turned to Madame Anselme. "My mother's very nice," she said, "but she worries too much."

"*Oui, Mademoiselle,*" the manager said, still smiling.

Something about the way Madame Anselme spoke made Amy wonder. "Peter Piper picked a peck of pickled peppers," she said quickly.

Madame Anselme continued to smile. "*Oui, Mademoiselle.*"

Amy smiled back. She was very happy to realize that Madame Anselme hadn't understood a word her mother had said.

four

Amy was pleased that the café across the street from their hotel looked just like the photographs of Parisian cafés in the guidebook. People were sitting at two rows of small tables, under a dark green awning that read CAFÉ CHOCOLAT. It sure made things a lot easier when French words resembled English. Next to the café was a newsstand, where Amy bought a French magazine. Then she and Monica found a vacant table and sat down.

Monica yawned. "I'm never going to recover from this jet lag if I don't have some coffee." Amy felt pretty much the same. She didn't like coffee, and she never drank it at home, but this wasn't home. She was ready to drink just about anything to feel more alert.

A waiter in a long white apron approached them and spoke. Amy was feeling too groggy to translate, but she imagined he was asking them what they wanted to order. *"Deux cafés, s'il vous plaît,"* she said, hoping he would understand that she was asking for two coffees. Since he nodded and didn't look particularly confused, she assumed that he did. And for the first time since arriving, she felt like she could take a deep breath, relax, and absorb the scene.

She couldn't believe it. She was sitting in a real Parisian café, watching the world go by, just like in the movies she'd seen in her French class. And it looked just the way it was supposed to look. People were sitting together chatting, or sitting alone reading the newspaper. The waiters weaved around the tables balancing trays, calling out cheery greetings of *"Bonjour, Madame"* and cheery goodbyes of *"Au revoir, Monsieur."* On the street, people bustled along, but they didn't have the frantic, stressed look Amy was accustomed to seeing in Los Angeles. A young girl walked by with a long, skinny loaf of bread in her arms. Two boys on skateboards whizzed past, expertly darting among the walkers. Some young people on bicycles rode along a special bicycle lane. But mostly, people were walking. Unlike Los Angeles, Paris was a walking city, and Amy was looking forward to covering every inch of it on foot.

Poor Monica didn't look like she was up for any walking, though. Her eyes were glazed over, and she kept putting a hand to her mouth to cover her yawns.

"Are you feeling okay?" Amy asked her.

"Sure, I'm just sleepy," Monica replied. "The coffee will wake me up."

It certainly did, before they even had a chance to drink it. As the waiter placed the tiny cups on their table, the smell alone was like a shot of adrenaline. Amy looked at the black liquid nervously and wondered how coffee this strong would affect a genetically enhanced clone. Would she have an exaggerated reaction? Could a cup of French coffee send her flying into space?

Monica was braver than Amy was. She actually brought the cup to her lips and took a sip. Then she began coughing violently. Immediately the waiter reappeared, with a knowing look on his face. "American?" he asked.

Monica managed to nod and cough at the same time. The man whisked away the coffees and returned seconds later with much larger cups, accompanied by a little pitcher of warm milk. Mixing some milk into her coffee, Amy took a tentative sip. She still didn't much like the stuff, but at least it tasted like the coffee back home.

As Monica drank her coffee, her eyes began to clear. "I'm feeling better already," she said. She fingered a lock of her hair, which had been dyed bluish black for the trip. "I must look awful, though."

"No, you don't," Amy assured her. "I think you look very pretty." She lowered her voice. "So does that guy over there."

"What guy?"

"Over there, just behind you and to the side. Dark hair, leather jacket. He's staring at you and drawing your picture."

Monica frowned, but there was no mistaking the glimmer of curiosity in her eyes. Very casually, she turned her head to get a peek at him. "Ooh, he's handsome. How can you see what he's drawing?"

Uh-oh, Amy thought. The jet lag was making her careless. Monica didn't know about her special talents, and Amy wasn't about to tell her. She liked and trusted her mother's friend, but Monica could be a little flaky. Amy knew she was going to have to watch herself on this trip.

Fortunately, Monica's thoughts didn't linger on Amy's

exceptional eyesight. She had opened her handbag and was furtively checking her appearance in a little compact mirror. The mirror served another purpose: It allowed Monica to get a better look at the guy. "Oh dear, he's coming over. We'd better not talk to strangers, Amy. This guy could be some sort of pickpocket. Hang on to your bag."

But the young man who approached them didn't appear to have any interest in their bags. Clutching a large white pad of paper, he smiled at Amy, but he addressed Monica.

"*Excusez-moi, Madame, j'espère que je ne vous dérange pas, mais je pense que vous êtes très belle.*"

Monica stared at him. "Huh?"

Amy wondered if she should tell Monica that this stranger thought she was beautiful. It turned out not to be necessary.

"*Pardon!*" the man said. "You do not speak French?"

"No," Monica said. "I'm American."

He inclined his head slightly, almost as if he was bowing. "Permit me to introduce myself. My name is Christophe, Christophe DuPont. I am an artist." As evidence of this, he showed Monica the drawing on his large pad.

Amy peered at the sketch. It wasn't a very good portrait.

Monica, on the other hand, seemed pleased. Then her smile disappeared, and she sighed. "I suppose you expect me to buy this from you."

The artist acted as if the mere thought horrified him. "Oh, no, *pas du tout*, not at all! I drew this for my own pleasure. I could never sell it. I will keep it always, to remind me of this very special moment. Such a delightful surprise! Here I sit in my regular morning café, and I see a beautiful woman! And her enchanting daughter," he added quickly, expanding his view to include Amy.

"I'm not her daughter," Amy said abruptly. She didn't care if she sounded rude. This guy was clearly a smooth talker, a real phony.

But apparently Monica didn't think so. "My name is Monica Jackson. And this is Amy Candler, the daughter of a friend of mine."

Monica extended her hand for a handshake, but Christophe turned it palm down and kissed the back of it. Then he swiveled in Amy's direction. Immediately Amy wrapped both hands firmly around her coffee cup and mumbled, "Hi." Monica invited Christophe Du-Pont to sit down, which he did.

"How are you enjoying Paris?" he asked.

"We just arrived this morning," Monica told him. "So we haven't seen much of Paris yet."

"From where in the United States do you come?" he asked.

"California," Monica replied. "Los Angeles. Do you know Los Angeles?"

"Of course! Hollywood, movie stars! I should have guessed you were from there. Are you an actress?"

Monica giggled. Amy wanted to gag. Her powers did not include fortune-telling, but she had no difficulty predicting Monica's immediate future. Hook, line, and sinker, Monica was going to fall for this guy, big-time. Amy supposed she couldn't blame her. Christophe DuPont was very good-looking, and he was positively dripping with gooey charm. Amy found it all kind of sickening, but she knew Monica went for that kind of flirty behavior. So much for her vow to remain man-free and dateless in Paris.

Monica was telling Christophe that she too was an artist, and they were clearly bonding. Amy had no desire to witness any more. She started to flip through the magazine she'd just bought. It was a weekly guide to what was going on in Paris, with listings of movies, plays, operas, art exhibits, and much more. Amy scanned the pages rapidly. She was looking for something in particular.

Several months ago, she'd gone to see a performance of *The Nutcracker* presented by a touring

French ballet company composed entirely of teen-agers. Amy had loved the ballet, but not just because the dancers were good. In fact, she'd paid attention only to one ballerina, a girl who was undoubtedly another Amy. It had been her first sighting of some-one like her—of someone cloned from the same genetic material she'd come from. She could still re-call the shock of watching a replica of herself on the stage.

As soon as the performance ended, she'd tried to get backstage to find the girl. But a meeting never took place. It had been a major disappointment.

Now here she was, in Paris, France, home of that ballet company. And searching the cultural listings in the magazine, she found it. Le Ballet de Jeunesse. She was in luck. The company was performing.

As she studied the performance dates, trying to re-member whether *jeudi* meant Tuesday or Thursday, she became aware of an odd prickling sensation on the back of her neck. It felt as though someone was watch-ing her. But Monica and her new friend were still flirt-ing outrageously and paying no attention to her. It had to be another symptom of jet lag.

But the feeling persisted and intensified. Instinctively Amy turned to look behind her.

A jolt of recognition whipped through her. She couldn't catch her breath. Her entire body was tingling; her head was spinning. Sitting at a table, looking directly at her, was someone she had never thought she would see again.

"Andy," she whispered.

f`i**5**ve

It wasn't jet lag. She was sure of that. There was nothing wrong with her eyes. Or his. They were azure beacons in a face that was just as shocked as hers. Their eyes locked, and for that moment nothing in the world could break their connection.

A flood of memories washed over her. Wilderness Adventure, the outdoor camping trip where they'd met. A boy with deep blue eyes and blond hair streaked with gold from the sun. A stream, promising cool refreshment, where he'd whipped off his T-shirt and jumped into the water—but not before revealing the crescent-moon birthmark on his right shoulder blade. A mark identical to the one on Amy's back.

She rose on unsteady feet, wondering why everyone at the café wasn't looking at her. Couldn't they hear her pounding heart? She could hear Andy's. . . .

His eyes drew her toward him. Then without warning, he broke the connection. He tossed some coins on the table, grabbed a notebook that was lying there, and hurried off.

"Andy!" Amy cried out, but all she could see was the resolute set of his shoulders as he moved swiftly to the street. "I'm going for a walk," she murmured, not sure if Monica heard her. She didn't care, either. There was only one thing on her mind—catching up with Andy.

He was already at the end of the street, waiting for the light to change so he could cross the intersecting boulevard. Amy took off, and as the light turned green, it required all her willpower not to exceed normal human running speed. Even so, she knew people were looking at her. Running along busy streets wasn't a common activity in Paris.

And it was even less common on the street Andy turned into. It was lined with covered stalls displaying everything from fish to fruit. She was so dazzled by the colors of the vegetables, the strong smells of the cheeses, that for a second she lost sight of Andy, way down at the end of the market.

But there he was, edging past a group of woman clustered around a stall overflowing with bananas. She hurried after him. "Andy!" she called again. She saw him pause, for what must have been only a hundredth of a second. Then he continued moving, faster now.

Amy ran, dodging the shoppers and trying not to crash into any stands. She was gaining on him. But someone at the banana stall must have sampled the goods. Amy slipped on a banana peel and fell.

A chorus of voices rang out, all asking in French if she was okay. She managed to answer, "Yes, I mean *oui,*" and got through the mob just in time to see Andy disappear down some stairs under a sign that read MÉT-ROPOLITAIN. That had to be the Métro, she thought. The Paris subway system. She raced down the steps after him and reached the bottom just as he put a ticket into a slot and passed through a turnstile.

Amy didn't have any Métro tickets, and she wasn't about to wait in line to purchase any. Not right now, anyway. Running to the turnstile, she was getting ready to hoist herself over when a harsh voice shouted, *"Ar-rêtez!"* She knew what that word meant. Stop. And she didn't have the opportunity to disobey the command.

Two large, strong hands were on her shoulders, pulling her away from the turnstile.

It was a police officer. She considered trying to break free from his grasp and making a dash for the train she heard pulling into the station. But it was useless. The man's grip was strong, and even if she could free herself, he'd come after her, maybe with a weapon. She had no idea how strict the French were about fare-beaters. Besides, it probably wasn't a great idea to break a law in a foreign country.

The policeman spoke sternly, and it wasn't hard to understand that he was scolding her. Speaking slowly and carefully in French, she told him she was a tourist, adding, *"Je ne sais pas comment voyager dans le Métro"*—she didn't know how to travel on the subway.

Either she sounded very honest or very stupid, but in any case the policeman let her go with instructions for buying Métro tickets. She didn't bother to get any, though. By now, Andy had to be long gone.

But why had he run from her in the first place? The answer was obvious. He didn't want to see her. He hated her for what she'd done to him, back at Wilderness Adventure.

They had been fleeing the camp when she spotted Mr. Devon, the mysterious man who kept turning up in her life at unexpected moments. He knew all about her being a clone, and he seemed to be watching out for her safety. He was on her side, protecting her from the organization. Or so she had believed.

Andy had disagreed. He called the man Mr. Devil and claimed that Mr. Devon was in cahoots with the organization. Amy had difficulty believing this, especially when Mr. Devon turned up dead. Murdered, actually. And everything had pointed to Andy as the killer. So she'd called the cops, and Andy had been taken away.

Later, she had come to realize that she'd been wrong about Andy. But it was too late. He had escaped from jail and disappeared from her life.

Yes, he had good reason to hate her, to distrust her. That had to be why he'd run from her. Unless . . .

The possibility hit her like a kick in the head. Unless the person she'd run after wasn't Andy. At least, not the Andy she knew, Andy Denker. After all, like her, he was a clone. There were other Amys in the world. There had to be other Andys, too. The person she saw running down into the subway could have been a replica, someone who'd never seen Amy before. And when Amy came after him, running and yelling, he could have been scared, thinking she was some kind of lunatic.

This was a definite possibility. But then why would he have been staring at her at the café? He wouldn't have known who she was. And would she have felt those intense emotions, that sense of connection, if he had been anyone but Andy Denker?

She had to find him. Closing her eyes, she searched her memory for a clue, something that might lead her to him. The notebook he'd grabbed when he took off had a label on it. She concentrated as hard as she could, dredging up every detail of the spiral pad, the green cover, the shreds in the binding where he must have torn out some pages, the faint stamp on the front of the notebook . . . She concentrated harder. Two words had been on the label. She drew her breath in sharply.

Lycée Internationale. She knew what a *lycée* was—the French version of a high school. Maybe he was a student there. As soon as she got back to the hotel, she'd ask Madame Anselme for a phone directory.

First, though, she had to go back to Café Chocolat. Monica was probably a basket case by now, thinking Amy was lost somewhere in Paris. For all Amy knew, there could be an entire police force out searching for her.

But Monica hadn't freaked out at all. She was still sitting at the same table, in the same position, with the same companion. When Amy joined them, Monica smiled vaguely as if Amy had only disappeared for seconds to use the rest room. And Christophe was still coming on to her with his fancy talk.

"You would do me such a great honor if you would join me this evening," he was telling Monica. "We can go to a fine restaurant, or perhaps to the Tuileries, where we can stroll in the garden."

Say yes, Amy ordered mentally. Getting rid of Monica for the evening meant she could start searching for the Lycée Internationale. Maybe Christophe would turn out to be a big plus. He was definitely an opportunist, but he was also someone who could distract Monica so that Amy could have more time on her own.

But Monica came back down to earth. "I'm sorry," she told Christophe with clear reluctance. "I'm responsible for Amy. I can't leave her alone, not on her first night in Paris."

"Of course not," Christophe said smoothly. "I am inviting the two of you! What would you like to do on your first night in Paris, Amy?"

She had an inspiration. "I want to go to the ballet," she said. "Le Ballet de Jeunesse. They're performing tonight." She looked in the magazine she'd left on the table. " 'Opéra Garnier,' " she read. "Do you know where that is?"

"But of course!" Christophe said. "We shall go to the ballet. If that is agreeable to you, Monique?"

"Her name is Monica," Amy reminded him.

"Ah yes, but a woman of such sophistication deserves a French name," Christophe replied.

Amy looked at Monica and made a face. But Monica had eyes only for Christophe.

It didn't matter. At least Amy had tonight to look forward to. And this time, she would find the dancing Amy.

six
6

From the outside, Opéra Garnier resembled a huge, extravagant golden wedding cake. The façade was covered with elaborate gilt designs and sculpted figures, and winged angels seemed to be flying alongside a big domed roof that looked like a crown. Even in New York, Amy had never seen anything quite so grand.

She flipped open her guidebook. "It took thirteen years to build this place," she told Monica and Christophe.

They weren't listening. "Do you go to the ballet often?" Monica was asking the new love of her life.

"Not very," Christophe said. "It is . . . how do you say in English?" He rubbed his thumb across two fingers.

"Very expensive." He smiled sadly. "I am a poor struggling artist."

"Well, we certainly don't expect you to pay for us," Monica assured him. "Believe me, I know what it's like to struggle as an artist. But you do like the ballet, don't you?"

"I am French, *chérie*. I appreciate all the fine arts."

Three wide avenues converged in front of the opera house. "Amy, take my hand," Monica said nervously, and Amy didn't object. The way the cars were speeding along, the street in front of Opéra Garnier looked more like a racetrack. "Why are they driving so fast?" she asked Christophe.

Again he smiled sickeningly. "They are French, *ma petite*."

So she was visiting a country where everyone was cultured and drove like a madman. Of course, she had to remind herself who was providing this information. She had a feeling that Christophe was prone to exaggeration. After all, he was already calling Monica *chérie*, darling, and he hadn't even known her for a full day. Amy herself wasn't too crazy about him calling her "my little one."

They made it across the busy intersection and into the grand entryway of the opera house. Amy tried not to stare at the other people streaming in. Everyone was dressed up, and the women looked perfectly groomed. Their clothes weren't fancy, but they were very elegant. Amy smoothed the front of her long flower-print skirt and hoped she didn't look out of place.

At the ticket booth, Christophe asked for three of the best seats available. When the man produced them, Christophe touched the pocket of his jacket and issued a soft moan.

"Oh dear. I seem to have forgotten my wallet."

"That's all right," Monica said. "I'll treat us all."

Amy did some rapid calculations, converting the French francs into dollars. These tickets weren't cheap. She hoped Christophe wasn't going to make a habit of forgetting his wallet, though he certainly seemed like the type who would. Back home, Amy had once seen a movie about a man who got women to buy him things. He was referred to as a gigolo. She had a feeling the part could easily have been played by Christophe DuPont.

They climbed a magnificently decorated marble staircase to get to their section, accepted programs from an usher, and found their seats. Amy looked around and noted that the place was filling rapidly. There had to be almost two thousand people in the five-tiered auditorium. It was nice to know this teen ballet company was doing so well, especially since one of the dancers was her clone.

She opened the program and began looking for the name. She found it almost immediately. Annie Perrault. She would be appearing in the first and third ballets.

The lights went down, the music began, the curtain went up, and Amy was immediately transported into another world. A dozen girls in soft white skirts floated across the stage, leaping lightly, spinning and twirling, moving in perfect synchronicity. They looked delicate and ethereal, but she knew how strong they had to be to perform all the intricate steps.

Then one of the dancers emerged from the line and did a short solo. Her feet in their pink toe shoes moved so fast they seemed to blur, and her leaps were so high that there was an audible gasp from the audience. Amy smiled. Despite the heavy makeup, which made all the girls on stage look pretty much alike, she knew who this one was.

Her heartbeat quickened. It wasn't an unfamiliar sensation. She'd experienced this before with Aimee Evans, the actress, and with Aly Kendricks, the reject clone who didn't have any powers. There were also the other Amys she'd seen—or *thought* she'd seen—in the New York City hospital. Each time, Amy had been so excited at the mere thought of meeting someone like her, of meeting in essence a sister. But every time, the encounter led to sadness or betrayal . . . even to danger.

Amy wasn't giving up, though. Someday she'd make a true heart-to-heart connection with another Amy. Maybe *this* was that day.

More dancers came onto the stage, and now Annie blended into the scene. Still, Amy didn't take her eyes off her. She didn't know much about ballet, but she didn't need to be an expert to know that Annie was incredibly talented. She had two more solos, and each time she danced superbly. Amy couldn't help feeling proud. At the end, she shouted, "Brava," with the rest of the audience when Annie took her solo bow.

As the applause subsided, Amy looked at the program. There would be an intermission now, followed by two more ballets. Again Amy noted that Annie was in the first one after the intermission but not the second. That meant she might be leaving before the performance was over. Amy had to find her now.

As soon as the lights came on, she told Monica she needed to find a rest room. Her search began. People were milling about in the lobby, and Amy had no idea which way to go. She spotted a uniformed man carrying a huge bouquet of roses wrapped in plastic. They had to be for one of the dancers. She followed the man down two flights of stairs and into a passageway.

There was a flurry of activity below. People carrying costumes and props rushed up and down the hallway. No one paid any attention to Amy. Some doors along the corridor were open, and she caught glimpses of dancers fixing their hair and touching up their makeup. At one of the doors, she stopped.

Six dancers sat at a counter, facing a mirror that ran the length of the wall. They were chatting as they applied their cosmetics. One of them was Annie Perrault.

Amy was a bundle of nerves. She didn't know how to approach Annie, or what to say. She didn't know if Annie knew about her own special talents. Or whether it was going to be a shock for her to see another girl who looked exactly like her.

Thinking about the previous disastrous encounters with other Amy clones, Amy didn't think she could go through it again. She was almost ready to back up and return to her seat, but it was too late.

Annie Perrault had seen Amy's reflection in the mirror. Her hand, clutching a brush, was frozen in midair. Amy could see the stunned expression on her face, and she steeled herself for whatever reaction Annie might have.

The last thing Amy expected to see was a smile. But that was what spread across Annie's face.

She rose from her seat and came out into the corridor. She looked at Amy steadily for a few seconds and then spoke in French. Amy had no problem at all understanding her.

"I knew this would happen someday," Annie was saying. "I prayed for it."

"You did?" Amy asked faintly.

Annie nodded. "You are American, yes? Then I will speak English." With her stage makeup and her hair in a bun, she looked older than Amy. But they had the exact same smile.

Annie continued in perfect English. "Ever since I learned about myself, I have been waiting to meet another like me. I hoped that perhaps one of us might see me in a performance. And here you are." She leaned forward and embraced Amy lightly, kissing her on both cheeks.

Amy hadn't been expecting this kind of reception. The warmth of Annie's greeting was overwhelming. "I'm—I'm so happy to find you," she said.

A woman at the end of the hall announced that it was time for the dancers to return to the stage. Annie spoke hurriedly. "I must go, but we will meet tomorrow, yes? Where can I find you?"

Amy told her the name of her hotel and its address.

"I will be there at ten o'clock tomorrow morning," Annie said. She pressed her lips against each of Amy's cheeks again. *"Au revoir!"* she called, and joined the other girls who were moving down the hall.

"Au revoir," Amy repeated faintly. It was a casual way of saying goodbye in France, and it meant something like "See you again" or "See you next time." Next time, meaning tomorrow. Amy couldn't believe the encounter had gone so well. Ecstatic, she sailed back upstairs to her seat, floating like a ballerina.

seven
7

Amy didn't think she'd be able to sleep at all that night. The lingering effects of jet lag and the excitement of the day, plus the unfamiliar bed, didn't promise a restful night, and she was afraid she'd be tossing and turning.

But she fell into a deep and dreamless sleep almost immediately. Even Monica's occasional snoring in the twin bed didn't bother her. When she woke up the next morning, Amy actually felt refreshed. And excited.

The prospect of spending the day with Annie Perrault almost drove thoughts of Andy out of her mind. Almost, but not quite. Questions hovered. Was it *her*

Andy she'd seen? If not, who? And why had the person run from her? Andy Denker might still be angry, but in that case, he would have confronted her, not fled from her. And any other Andy wouldn't have known who she was, and couldn't possibly be fearful of a girl who was four years younger and half his size. Maybe Annie would know if there were any Andy clones in Paris.

Amy went into the bathroom to shower, and when she came out Monica was sitting up in bed. She too looked like she'd had an excellent sleep. "Good morning," she said brightly. "Can you believe we're waking up in Paris, France?"

"Yeah, it's unbelievable, isn't it?" Amy turned away so Monica couldn't see her face. Another troubling thought had just hit her.

Annie would be arriving at the hotel very soon. Monica would have to meet her. How was Amy going to explain their physical resemblance? Without stage makeup, Monica would have to be practically blind not to see that they were identical.

Monica had gone into the bathroom. "I'll meet you downstairs," Amy called, and ran out the door. She dialed her mother's hotel from the lobby pay phone, but the receptionist told her that Madame Candler was not in her room at the moment. Would Mademoiselle Candler like to leave a message?

"*Merci, non,*" Amy said. She hung up and pondered the situation. She'd have to come up with a story for Monica all by herself.

But that turned out not to be necessary. Annie appeared.

"I am early, I know," she said, her brown eyes sparkling. "I could not wait any longer! I am so happy to find you!"

Once again, Amy was overcome with her warmth. "Me too," she said. "I'm happy to find *you!*" She glanced at the stairs. There was no sign of Monica, but she'd be coming down very soon. In a rush, Amy explained the situation to Annie.

Annie listened intently. Then she asked, "Will this Monica person talk to your mother frequently this week?"

"I don't think so," Amy said. "My mom's in meetings all day, and when she calls here, we'll probably be out. Monica's so gaga about this guy she met, she won't even think about calling her."

Annie's brow furrowed. "Gaga? That means a little senile in French."

"Really? In English it means crazy about someone," Amy said. "*Monica est tombée amoureuse d'un homme,*" she added. To say "She's falling in love with a man" seemed kind of bland, but at least Annie understood and nodded sagely.

"Then she will not pay much attention to us."

"True," Amy admitted. "But we'll still need to explain why we look alike."

As she'd expected, without makeup Annie could be her twin. Her hair was longer, and the physical exercise of her dancing had made her more slender than Amy, but even so . . .

"I have an idea," Annie said. When she explained it to Amy, Amy was impressed. Annie's quick thinking proved that Annie was an Amy. At that moment, Madame Anselme noticed them and was clearly taken aback by their resemblance. In French, they tried out their story on her, and the hotel manager bought it.

By the time Monica came down to the lobby, they were completely prepared. As Monica gaped at the two of them, Amy explained.

"It's so incredible! My mom had the name of a distant relative who lives here in Paris, and this is her daughter, Annie."

"*Bonjour,*" Annie chimed in. "I am very excited to see the cousin I have never met."

"We're only, like, third cousins or something," Amy said, "but we look almost exactly alike!"

"You really do," Monica agreed. "This is uncanny. But maybe it's not that uncommon. After all, you do share some of the same genes."

Amy held back a giggle.

"I'm starving," Monica said. "Let's get some breakfast. How do you say that in French?"

"*Petit déjeuner*," Annie told her. "Is there a café near here?"

"Just across the street," Amy said, and they proceeded out the door. She wasn't at all surprised to see Christophe DuPont already waiting at Café Chocolat. In her opinion, he overdid his show of joy at seeing them.

"Monique, *chérie*, you bring out the sun on a cloudy day!"

Amy looked knowingly at Annie, who nodded with understanding. Clearly, she'd figured out that this was Monica's new love.

Monica introduced Annie, and again the girls told the story that would explain their identical appearance. Christophe accepted it as easily as Monica had, and they sat down with him. He ordered *le petit déjeuner* for all, and within seconds, the waiter delivered their coffee and crescent-shaped rolls, which Amy knew were called *croissants*.

Monica had taken out her guidebook. "Christophe, which are your favorite museums in Paris? I want to introduce Amy to some truly great art."

Christophe uttered a disparaging laugh. "I have no

favorite museum here, *chérie*. They show only the tired old classic paintings. Monet, Matisse, Picasso . . ." He waved a hand in the air as if to dismiss them all.

"But those are all important artists," Amy said. Even she knew that.

Christophe gave her a condescending smile. "You are a child, you know nothing of art. Those artists, they are all dead." To Monica he said, "Please, allow me the privilege of giving you all an education in art, of introducing you to the exciting new art of today."

Monica didn't require much convincing. "That sounds wonderful. What could be better than seeing art with a real Parisian artist? What do you think, Amy?"

Amy looked at Annie and hoped she would pick up on what Amy was about to say. "Actually, Monica, I'd rather see some of the famous sights today. You know, like the Eiffel Tower."

Annie didn't disappoint her. "I can show you those sights," she said. "That way Monica and Monsieur Du-Pont can look at art."

Unfortunately, Monica remembered her responsibilities. "I think we should stay together, Amy. If you really want to go to the Eiffel Tower, we'll go there."

Amy wasn't going to give up that easily. "Why don't I find a pay phone and call my mom? I'm sure she'll say it's okay for me to go around with Annie."

"Christophe, do you have a mobile phone?" Monica asked. He produced one, and Amy took it. Holding it so Monica couldn't see, she pretended to punch in some numbers.

"*Bonjour. Madame Candler, s'il vous plaît.*" She paused and silently counted to five. "Hello, Mom? Annie Perrault is here with me, and she wants to show me Paris. Is it okay if I go with her and Monica does something else?"

One, two, three, she counted silently. "Okay, thanks, Mom."

"Let me speak to her," Monica said.

"Mom, Monica wants to—oh, okay, I'll tell her." She handed the phone back to Christophe. "She had to run off to a meeting. But she said it was fine for me to sightsee with Annie."

"I know Paris very well," Annie assured Monica. "I'm a Parisian, after all."

Monica looked at Christophe. "Is it safe for young girls to explore Paris on their own?"

He shrugged. "But of course."

Amy had suspected that would be his answer. Still, she had to be grateful that Monica was now sufficiently reassured and gave her permission for Amy and Annie to go off by themselves.

They arranged to meet up again at four that afternoon, on a street corner in the area called Montmartre.

"What would you like to do first?" Annie asked Amy as they left the café.

"Ask you a million questions," Amy replied immediately.

Annie smiled. "The same is true for me. I want to know everything about you. But you are the visitor to my city, so you may ask the first question."

"How did you find out about yourself?" Amy demanded.

"I have always known that I am adopted. My parents told me when I was very young that they had taken me from an orphanage. But I became concerned about this a year ago. I wanted to know what kind of people my real father and mother were. My parents knew nothing, so my father hired a detective to investigate. When he returned with the story of Project Crescent, my father did not believe him. But something happened to convince us."

"What was that?"

"I was practicing a lift in my ballet class. The foolish boy who held me was very weak, and he dropped me."

"Ouch," Amy said sympathetically. Being a clone didn't make a person free from pain.

"Yes, I broke my leg, and I was taken to the hospital. By the time a doctor examined me—"

Amy guessed the rest. "Your leg was completely healed."

"Precisely! Now it is my turn. Why was Project Crescent terminated?"

Amy explained. "When the scientists learned the real goals of the project, they stopped it."

"The real goals?"

"The organization behind the project wanted to create a master race, a nation of perfect people."

Annie frowned. "I do not understand. Why did the scientists object to this?"

"Because it's wrong! A master race might try to take over the world and destroy all people who aren't the same as them. Like the Nazis tried to do."

"The Nazis," Annie repeated.

"Yes, the Nazis. You know who they were, don't you?"

"Of course, this is a part of French history. In 1940 Nazi Germany attacked France, and the Nazis occupied our country for four years."

Amy thought that must have been awful, and she was mildly surprised that Annie spoke of it so nonchalantly. But Annie hadn't been alive back then, so maybe it was all just boring history to her. Amy herself had to admit that she could never get all that excited when she was taught about the California Gold Rush.

"I do not understand something," Annie went on. "How could they create a race with only female clones? Why did they not make male clones too?"

Amy hesitated. "I'm not sure," she said finally. "Maybe they just didn't get to that part." So Annie didn't know about the Andys.

And Amy decided not to say anything. Not yet, at least. After all, what did she really know, anyway? Only what Andy had told her back at Wilderness Adventure. Which wasn't much. "Where are we going?" she asked Annie. They had reached the river.

"I am taking you to the islands," Annie said.

"Islands? What islands?"

"There are two islands in the River Seine," Annie told her. "The Île de la Cité and the Île St.-Louis. On the Île de la Cité, there is Notre-Dame, the great cathedral."

"What's on the Île St.-Louis?" Amy asked.

Annie grinned. "Only the most wonderful ice cream in all the world."

They started with the Île de la Cité. Notre-Dame was magnificent, and Amy was stunned to learn that construction on the cathedral had begun in the twelfth century. Columbus hadn't even found America yet. She also saw La Conciergerie, which dated from the tenth century.

"It was a prison during the French Revolution," Annie told her. "Prisoners were kept here until they were taken to the guillotine."

"To the what?"

"The guillotine. A contraption with a sharp blade that cut off their heads."

"Gross!"

"But it was very democratic," Annie assured her. "Even kings and queens died on the guillotine. Of course, we do not have it anymore. It is too bad."

Amy was startled. "Why?"

"There are many who deserve to be guillotined," Annie said. "Look at those people over there."

Amy looked. A cluster of men and women were climbing down the steps of a tour bus and began taking photos. From the way they were dressed, in shorts and sneakers, it was obvious that they were on vacation. "What about them?"

Annie spoke decisively. "They should all be executed for having bad fashion sense."

Amy couldn't help laughing.

Then she stopped and drew in her breath sharply.

"What is it?" Annie asked.

Amy was looking at the back of a guy's blond head. He wore a T-shirt and blue jeans. When he turned slightly, Amy got a glimpse of his face.

"Nothing," she said. "I just thought I saw someone I

knew. But it wasn't him. Hey, where do we get that wonderful ice cream?" Maybe a couple of scoops would chase Andy out of her mind for a while.

They crossed over to the other island and headed directly to Berthillon's, the place Annie said made the best ice cream in the world. There was a long line, but Annie entertained Amy by whispering jokes about the people around them.

"Look at that man. There should be a law forbidding fat people from eating ice cream. And see that woman over there?" she said, nodding in the woman's direction. "You can see that she is not really French."

"How can you tell? She's speaking French."

"But look at her hair! No self-respecting French woman would ever leave her home with such messy hair. Oh, and that poor girl there . . . if I had a face like that, I would dig a hole in the ground and hide in it forever!"

Annie's comments struck Amy as almost cruel, but even so, she couldn't help laughing. Annie had a way of making everything seem so funny.

And she was right about the ice cream. It was better than any ice cream Amy had tasted before. The two girls licked their cones as they strolled along the elegant residential streets and then across a bridge to the

Right Bank. Annie pointed out the Eiffel Tower, way off in the distance.

"We could go there, if you like, and climb all the way to the top. Or perhaps there is something else you would prefer to do."

Amy considered the possibilities. Then she remembered something she'd read in the guidebook. "Do you know where the Catacombs are?"

Annie stared at her for a minute. "Yes, I have been there before. Why do you want to go to the Catacombs?"

Amy shrugged. "I don't know, my guidebook made them sound kind of neat and creepy. But we don't have to go there, if it doesn't interest you."

"Oh no, I don't mind at all," Annie said. "I like the Catacombs. In fact, it is one of my favorite places in Paris. Come, we can take the Métro just over there."

The word *Métro* brought thoughts of Andy rushing back. Even though Amy knew there were many different Métro lines, she couldn't help looking around for him as they waited on the underground platform. And when the train rushed into the station, she searched the windows for a passenger with deep blue eyes and blond hair.

"I hope they sell postcards at the Catacombs," she said, trying to distract herself. "I went to send one back home to Eric. He's my boyfriend." She knew she was really saying that to remind herself that she already had a boyfriend.

They changed trains once, and she forced herself not to look around for Andy anymore. Finally they arrived at their stop and quickly made their way aboveground. "The entrance to the Catacombs is just across the street," Annie said. She pointed to a spot where a group of people were standing. "I think that a guided tour is about to begin."

She was right. As they joined the group, a solemn-faced man was introducing himself. "Good day, my name is Sébastien, and I will be your guide to the Paris Catacombs." He looked at Annie and then at Amy, and nodded. "Please follow me. And do not stray from the group."

He was speaking in French, and Amy realized to her pleasure that she had no problem at all understanding him. It had just taken her a little time to get accustomed to the voices and accents here. But as the guide led them along a spiral stone staircase, she wondered if understanding French was such a good thing in a situation like this. Sébastien was explaining why it was so important not to leave the group.

"There are one hundred and eighty miles of underground tunnels," he said. "There is no light source other than the one I carry. It would be very easy to lose one's way. In 1793, a man named Philibert Aspairt came down here to explore. Eleven years later, topographical workers discovered his body." He paused. "I often imagine Aspairt's agony as he must have groped and stumbled in the darkness, searching for an exit. His death, from starvation, was surely slow and painful."

The group fell silent, and Amy shivered. It wasn't a pleasant tale, and Sébastien's low, melancholy voice made it even creepier.

They had reached the bottom of the stairs and now stood in a small gallery, dimly lit by Sébastien's lantern. "We are now twenty-five meters under the surface of Paris," Sébastien intoned. He led them into a dark tunnel, and they all walked in silence for a while. Then they came to what looked like a cave opening. He pointed to a sign and read the French words out loud. " 'Arrêtez! C'est ici l'empire de la mort.' "

It sounded creepy in French, and it was even creepier in English. "Stop! Here is the empire of the dead."

eght

"The tunnels were created in Roman times, when limestone was excavated from underground," Sébastien said. "In 1786, Parisian cemeteries were overcrowded, and the areas surrounding them had become unhealthy. It was decided to move the bones of those buried in the cemeteries to these tunnels. You are about to view the remains of seven million Parisians."

Even with those ominous words, Amy wasn't prepared for what she was about to see. They entered a gallery lined with the remnants of various body parts of former human beings. A collective gasp erupted from the group as they faced walls made up of bones and skulls.

They moved slowly. Amy could hear the wet gravel beneath her feet. And no one spoke—as if it would be rude to disturb the dead. Amy couldn't remember ever seeing anything so eerie before in her life. In some galleries, the bones were just piled in heaps. But in other galleries, the piles were very orderly, with bones of a particular body part lined up side by side, then topped with bones from another part. They formed patterns, these bones, like intricate weavings, topped with skulls for decoration.

As she looked at these masses of bones, particularly the skulls, Amy tried to envision them as people, but it was impossible. Still, they had all been flesh and blood once. Each skull represented a human being with a face and a personality, with unique features and feelings. But to look at them now, you couldn't know which were men and which were women . . . who was young, who was old . . . who was fat or thin, pretty or ugly. Down here, everyone was equal.

Dimly Amy became aware of the sound of dripping water from above. She looked up and saw stalactites hanging from the ceiling. It made the whole experience of the Catacombs seem otherworldly.

She didn't know how Annie could call this one of her

favorite places in Paris, and she was grateful when Sébastien began speaking again.

"What you are seeing is only a small portion of the Catacombs," he said. "Miles of tunnels exist under Paris, but the public is not allowed to visit them. It would be too complicated to keep track of everyone. To make sure no one got lost. So the police have sealed the entrances."

Amy had been eager to visit the Catacombs, but now that she was here, she didn't know who would want to sneak into this labyrinth of tunnels on their own.

Sébastien continued. "During World War Two, the German occupation forces had a communications center in the Catacombs. Interestingly, the French Resistance, the group which actively fought the Nazis, also made use of the Catacombs and held their secret meetings here. Yet there is no evidence that the two opposing groups ever encountered each other. This demonstrates how vast and tangled the underground network is."

Amy found this historic fact fascinating. Having good guys and bad guys roaming these tunnels, hiding from each other, seemed very dramatic, even a little romantic. Now she looked around with more interest and less fear.

Even so, she was glad when the tour ended and they

went back up to the surface. The gray sky was like brilliant sunshine after the gloom below.

"Did you enjoy that?" Annie asked her.

Amy didn't want to let on how she'd felt underground. She didn't want Annie to think she frightened easily. That would be so—un-clone-like. "Oh, it was great," she said. "Really great."

The girls ate a late lunch, during which Amy was introduced to the popular French sandwich the *croquemonsieur*. It was like a grilled ham and cheese, and it was totally delicious. By the time they finished, Annie said they had to get moving if they were going to meet Monica and Christophe on time.

"At this moment, we are in the south of Paris," she told Amy. "Montmartre is at the farthest northern point."

But it didn't take them long to get from one end of Paris to the other on the speedy Métro. They even reached Montmartre early, which allowed them to climb what seemed like hundreds of steps to get a spectacular view of Paris. The climb down was much faster, and soon they were in a square, surrounded by little shops and cafés. Artists had set up easels and were offering to paint portraits of the tourists.

They reached the designated corner at precisely the same time that Monica and Christophe arrived. "What did you girls do today?" Monica asked them.

When Amy reached the part about the Catacombs, Christophe smirked. "But you took the guided tour. You did not see the real Catacombs."

"The guide told us the public isn't allowed in the other tunnels," Amy replied. "He said the entrances are all sealed."

"*Some* entrances are sealed," Christophe acknowledged. "But if one knows where to go, one can get into the forbidden Catacombs."

"Why would you *want* to go in them?" Amy asked. She looked at Annie, who was listening to Christophe with obvious interest.

"Have you been in the forbidden Catacombs?" Annie asked him

"I have not toured the entire network," he said. "But there is an area where I go quite frequently to meet fellow artists."

Incredulous, Amy asked, "You *paint* down there?"

"Not exactly," Christophe said. "It is a place for social gatherings."

Amy was dubious. The Catacombs didn't look like Party Central to her.

At that moment, a church bell struck four. "I must go now," Annie said. "There is a performance tonight."

"A performance?" Monica asked. "Of what?"

"Annie is in the ballet company we saw last night," Amy told her. "Isn't that a wild coincidence?"

Fortunately, Monica was the kind of person who believed in coincidences. "You girls were fated to meet!"

"Can we get together tomorrow?" Amy asked Annie.

Annie nodded. "You could meet me after school, if you like."

"Great," Amy said. "Just tell me when and where."

Annie took a pad of paper out of her bag and wrote on it. "This is the address of my school," she said. "Can you be there at four-thirty?"

"Absolutely." They embraced and did the cheek-kissing thing again. Then Annie ran off toward the Métro.

"She seems like a very nice girl," Monica said.

"She's a lot of fun," Amy agreed. She looked at the paper Annie had given her. Her eyes widened.

Above the address were written the words *Lycée Internationale*.

The same words she'd seen stamped on Andy's notebook.

nine

Amy looked at her watch. She and Monica had planned to visit three museums today. They'd started with the Louvre, at ten o'clock that morning. It was now four o'clock, and they were still there.

This was hardly surprising. The Louvre was the largest museum in Paris, and six hours later they had yet to cover half of it. Despite what Christophe had told them yesterday, the work of the old dead artists was amazing. From the beautiful entrance—a huge glass pyramid—on through to the many rooms of art and antiquities, Amy had been captivated. It only confirmed for her that Christophe was a fool. The Louvre was thrilling.

And now Amy was ready for the possibility of another thrill—seeing Andy. "I have to go meet Annie now," she told Monica. "Do you want to come with me?" She crossed her fingers behind her back and didn't release them until Monica replied.

"No thanks, Amy, I'm meeting Christophe. We'll wait for you at Café Chocolat."

Amy took off. Outside the museum, she found a pay phone and dialed the number of her mother's hotel. Of course, Nancy wasn't there. Since their arrival in Paris, they'd been missing each other's phone calls. Amy was sorry she hadn't been able to tell her about Annie. She hurried to the Métro and took it to the Left Bank stop that Annie had told her to go to. From there she followed the map to the street where the Lycée Internationale stood. It wasn't a long walk, and from the lack of people milling around the building, she knew the students hadn't even been dismissed yet.

Hoisting herself up onto a low wall, Amy watched the doors. She took deep breaths to calm her nerves. It was only minutes, but it seemed like hours before the doors opened and students began to emerge. With her exceptional vision, she was able to scan the faces rapidly.

Her breath caught when she spotted Andy. He was with two other students, and they were deep in conversation. He didn't even see her.

She let the group pass and then slipped off the wall. Silently she followed them.

At the end of the street, one of the students left the group. Half a block farther, Andy and the third student parted ways. Now Andy was alone.

He turned and went through a wide entrance into a vast garden. Amy glanced at her map. This was the Luxembourg Garden. Still keeping a safe distance, she followed Andy past the formal flower beds to a large fountain. People sat in chairs around the garden, enjoying the tranquil atmosphere.

Andy sat down in one of the chairs and opened a book. Amy quickened her step.

"Hello, Andy."

He looked up, and his face went pale. It wasn't a blank expression, though. He knew exactly who she was. She could see it in his eyes.

"Don't run away," Amy pleaded. "Please talk to me."

He didn't move, but he wasn't receptive. "I don't know who you are."

"Yes, you do, Andy. You looked up when I called your name."

"My name *is* Andy. But I don't know you." He closed his book and got up. "Excuse me, I have to go."

Amy wasn't about to let that happen. In those brief seconds that they'd been face-to-face, a feeling of electricity had shot through her, entering every pore of her skin. This was *her* Andy. There was absolutely no doubt in her mind.

She remained by his side, keeping up with him as he strode through the garden. "What are you doing in Paris?"

"I'm an exchange student. I'm spending a year at a school here."

"The Lycée Internationale, I know. What are you studying?"

He stared straight ahead. "French language and history."

"Did you hear what happened to Willard?"

For a brief second he seemed to hesitate. Then he straightened his shoulders. "Who?"

"Willard, the boy who was at Wilderness Adventure with us. Remember, he helped Dallas carry Flora's body to the main road? He never returned, and we thought Dallas had killed him. Well, he escaped in the woods."

"I have no idea what you're talking about," he said stiffly.

"I don't know what happened to Brooke," Amy went on.

"Who?"

"Brooke, the girl from San Francisco."

He said nothing. They walked along in silence.

"Do you still practice karate?" she asked. "I remember how you fought that mountain wolf."

"What mountain wolf? It was a bear—" He stopped.

"That's right," Amy said softly. "It was a bear. He grabbed me. You fought him off with karate moves."

He was silent. Then, quietly, he corrected her. "Kick boxing."

"That's right," Amy said again. She touched his arm. He turned and faced her. Now she could see the tiniest tear glistening in his eye.

"Oh, Andy."

Then, almost as if it was against his will, he opened his arms, and she fell into them. For at least a full minute they held each other, neither of them moving, neither trying to break free.

Amy had to speak. "I'm sorry," she whispered. "I'm sorry I thought you killed Mr. Devon. I'm sorry I called the police."

"I understand," he murmured.

She lifted her head so she could look him in the eyes.

"Why did you run away when you saw me the other day?"

His eyes were serious. "I really am here as an exchange student, Amy. I want to spend this year living as a regular student, a normal person. I don't want anyone to know I'm different. I've almost made myself forget who I am! Then I saw you at that café. And I had to remember."

"Annie hasn't made you remember?"

He looked truly puzzled. "Who?"

"Annie Perrault. She—she's like me."

He still looked blank.

"She goes to the Lycée Internationale, Andy. You must have seen her."

"It's a big school, Amy. And if she's your age, that means she's four grades under me. We wouldn't even have our classes on the same halls."

That made sense. Then Amy remembered why she had come to the Lycée Internationale. "Ohmigod, I was supposed to meet Annie in front of the school at four. Come with me, Andy."

He gazed at her intently. "On one condition. Don't tell her about me, okay? I want to go on like I am."

"I won't say anything," Amy promised him.

Together they hurried back to the Lycée Internationale. There were still a few students lingering in front of the school. One of them was Annie. And she didn't look happy.

"Amy, where have you been? You are late. It is nearly five o'clock!" Then she saw Andy, and her mouth shut.

"I'm so sorry, Annie. I ran into Andy Decker, and it was such a surprise! Andy and I met at survival camp back in Oregon. Now he's an exchange student at the Lycée Internationale! Isn't that a coincidence?"

"Yes, that certainly is a coincidence," Annie said, looking at Andy. "How do you do? I am Annie Perrault."

"Pleased to meet you," Andy said.

"Will you be joining us for a walk?" Annie asked him politely.

"Sure," Andy said. "Thanks."

An awkward silence descended on the group as they walked toward the river. Amy attempted to break it. "What kind of school is the Lycée Internationale?" she asked.

"It is a special high school for children of foreign diplomats, and exchange students from other countries," Annie told her. "There are also those like myself, who are working in artistic professions and who require special schedules. Classes are offered in several languages, and at flexible times."

"That's good," Amy said. "Where are we going today?"

"I would like to show you the Place de la Concorde," Annie said.

"Okay." Amy looked over at Andy. He looked tense. "Do you want to see the Place de la Concorde, Andy?"

"Sure," he said. "You shouldn't miss seeing it."

Annie gave them lots of information about Paris as they walked. "This bridge is called the Pont Neuf," she told them as they crossed the river to the Right Bank. "That means 'new bridge,' which is ironic, because it is the oldest bridge of all those that cross the Seine."

"Really?" Amy said. "Isn't that interesting, Andy?"

"Yes," he said. "Very interesting."

Amy couldn't understand why they were all talking so stiffly. She thought that perhaps French people were just more formal with strangers than Americans were. But Andy was being just as formal as Annie. Maybe he was afraid of slipping up and revealing something about himself. Or maybe he was just being shy.

They walked on past the Louvre and through the Tuileries gardens. Amy tried to keep a conversation going, but Annie and Andy didn't seem to warm up to each other. They weren't hostile—they just weren't friendly.

When they reached the Place de la Concorde, Annie explained the significance of the spot. "This was where the guillotine stood," she told them. "After the Revolution, during the Reign of Terror, over a thousand people were executed right here, including Marie Antoinette and the king, Louis the Sixteenth."

It was hard to envision heads being chopped off in the middle of this busy spot, with its monuments and fountains, and cars whizzing around them. Almost as hard as trying to picture the skulls in the Catacombs as real people.

"Annie and I went to the Catacombs yesterday," she told Andy. "Have you been there?"

"No," Andy said.

"You should. It's creepy but really amazing. Did you know that the German Nazis and the French Resistance both held meetings down there during World War Two? And that they never ran into each other?"

"I've heard that," Andy said. "One of the secret entrances to the Catacombs was just under the Lycée Internationale."

"That is not correct," Annie said sharply. "It is only a legend."

"No, it's true," Andy insisted. "I'm taking a course right now about the history of the Occupation, and there's a map in one of my books that shows the entrances. The teacher says it's sealed up."

Annie didn't say anything, but her lips tightened and her eyes narrowed. Amy couldn't blame her for being irritated. It had to be annoying to hear a foreigner spout French history as well as a native French person. It certainly didn't improve things between Annie and Andy.

Amy didn't know what to do. She felt a real bond with Annie. As for Andy, she couldn't deny the sparks and the deep connection between them.

"Do you guys have plans for tonight?" Andy asked suddenly.

Amy looked at Annie, but Annie didn't meet her eyes. She was staring at the garden-lined avenue straight ahead. "This is the Champs-Elysées. It leads to the Arc de Triomphe, the 'Triumphant Arch,' commissioned by Napoleon in 1806 to celebrate a battle victory."

"Nice," Amy said.

Andy repeated his question. "Would you guys like to do something tonight?"

Annie turned to him. "I am busy," she said. "I have a ballet rehearsal."

"What about you, Amy?"

Amy gazed straight ahead at the Arc de Triomphe and couldn't deny a feeling of triumph. "I'm free," she said.

ten 10

Amy was surprised to find Monica alone at Café Chocolat when she and Andy arrived. "Where's Christophe?" she asked.

"He went to buy tickets for a concert tonight," Monica replied. "A French rap group! I won't understand a word, but Christophe promised to translate for us."

"Us?"

"Yes, you'll come too, won't you?"

Amy bit her lip. "Uh, I'm not sure. Monica, this is Andy Denker. We met him on a camping trip in Oregon. He's here in Paris as an exchange student."

"Hi, Andy. Do you want to come to the rap concert? Maybe we can get an extra ticket at the door."

Amy looked at Andy and hoped he could see in her eyes that a loud concert wasn't exactly her idea of a perfect evening.

"I don't want to intrude," Andy said smoothly. "Amy and I wanted to hang out tonight, but if you've already made plans—"

"I'm sure Christophe can return my ticket," Amy broke in. "Tell the truth, Monica, wouldn't you like to be alone with him? You don't really want me tagging along, and neither does he."

Monica's face went pink, but she shook her head. "That's not true, Amy. I'm always happy to have you with us. And Christophe adores you!"

Amy looked at her dubiously. "He does?" All she could think was that the feeling wasn't exactly mutual.

"Oh yes, he thinks you're an enchanting girl. He's always asking about you."

Amy didn't particularly like the sound of that, but she wasn't sure why. Monica looked at her watch. "I wonder what's taking him so long. He should be back by now."

Suddenly Amy wondered if Christophe had borrowed money for the tickets from Monica, and if he was leaving town at that very moment. It sounded like the kind of thing a gigolo would do.

But for once, she had misjudged the man. Seconds later Christophe appeared at the café. "I am so sorry, there are no more tickets available for the concert. Perhaps you will allow me to take you lovely ladies to a fine French film this evening." Then he noticed Andy.

Amy introduced them and said, "You and Monica can go to the film, Christophe. Andy and I have other plans."

"Oh, and what are your plans?" Christophe asked, seeming more than just casually curious.

Andy wasn't intimidated by his tone. "I'd like to take Amy on a *bâteau-mouche* tonight," he said.

"A *what*?" Monica asked.

Christophe laughed the laugh that indicated his disapproval. "A *bâteau-mouche* is an excursion boat which sails the River Seine. It is for the purpose of sightseeing, a very touristic thing to do. No self-respecting Parisian would go on a *bâteau-mouche*."

"Well, lucky for me, I'm not a self-respecting Parisian," Amy declared. "I'd love to take a tour on a *bâteau-mouche*, Andy."

"Great," Andy said. He turned to Monica. "You won't need to worry, it's not dangerous. I'll watch out for Amy and get her back to the hotel safely. And not too late."

"I suppose that's all right," Monica said. "And I *would* like to see a French movie. Christophe, you'll translate for me, won't you?"

Christophe didn't reply. He looked a little annoyed, but he recovered quickly. "Perhaps I am a bit hasty to condemn the *bâteau-mouche*. After all, I myself have never taken a boat tour. This could be an educational experience for me." He blessed Amy and Andy with a smile. "Monica and I shall accompany you on your voyage tonight."

Amy noted that he didn't ask Monica's opinion. The notion of having two chaperones with them was not appealing. What was the deal with Christophe anyway? If he was really interested in Monica, why in the world would he want a couple of teenagers hanging out with them? This didn't make any sense to her at all. And there was still so much she wanted to talk about, privately, with Andy.

A few hours later, the four of them were waiting for the *bâteau-mouche*. They were all forced to listen patiently as Christophe described the trials and tribulations of an unappreciated struggling artist in Paris, and although Monica didn't seem to mind, Amy could only hope that Andy was doing what *she* was doing—channeling all her powers to block out the man's voice.

She was pleasantly surprised when the boat approached the dock. It was much bigger than she had anticipated. They went on board and took seats together, but as soon as the boat began to move, she and Andy looked at each other in complete understanding.

They rose. "We're going to walk around," Andy said firmly, and before Christophe could make any suggestion about joining them, he and Amy escaped.

"That guy's a jerk," Andy announced.

"No kidding," Amy said. "Monica's always falling for the wrong men, but this one's the worst. He's always talking about himself, he won't pay for anything, and he's full of meaningless compliments."

"Well, let's forget about him now." Andy leaned against the railing. "It's nice out tonight, isn't it?"

But Amy was still thinking about Christophe. "He gives me the creeps. Do you think he's just trying to get money from Monica? And why is he interested in me?"

"I don't know," Andy said.

"What did you think of Annie?" Amy asked him. "I really like her."

"That's nice," Andy said.

"I got the feeling you weren't too crazy about her. How come?"

Andy groaned. "Can we talk about something else? Or maybe not talk at all? Amy, look around you! We're in Paris, the City of Light!"

For the first time, Amy realized why the city had that nickname. She fell silent as she took in the scene that surrounded them. All the buildings along the Seine were illuminated. The lights cast a spellbinding aura over the city. Paris was beautiful by day, but at night it was beyond spectacular. The elegant old buildings that lined the river took on a golden glow. She recognized Notre-Dame, its spires soaring, almost touching the sky, and the Palais de Justice, which looked like a castle out of a fairy tale. No wonder there were so many songs about Paris, so many movies set here. She was overcome with a sense of beauty, magic, and romance.

She couldn't be sure, though, if that last sensation came from the lights and the city or the feeling of Andy's hand on hers.

"Look at the Eiffel Tower," Andy said.

Annie had pointed it out to her yesterday. But at night it was something else altogether. The golden lights made the tower seem to glow from within. Words like *spectacular, breathtaking*—none seemed adequate to describe it. An image of a movie her French teacher had shown in class popped into her mind. The final scene was set at the top of the Eiffel Tower, where a man and a woman kissed.

Andy whispered in her ear. "Did you ever see a French movie called *L'amour dans la Tour*?"

Amy caught her breath. *"Love in the Tower!* I was just thinking of that!"

His hand tightened on hers, and now she too felt as if she was all aglow.

eleven

The next morning Amy woke before Monica again, but this time she didn't rush to get into the shower. She wanted to lie in silence for a few minutes and enjoy the waves of contentment that washed over her.

Last night with Andy had been perfect. And this would be a perfect day. Andy had told her it was a holiday in France—he didn't know which one, because there was a holiday practically every other week and it was hard to keep track of them all. But whatever special day this was, it meant no school, and she and Andy would have the whole day together. She knew that Monica and Christophe had their own plans. She'd heard him last night, telling her about some kind of party he wanted to take her to. She and Andy would be on their own.

Amy felt unbelievably happy. After Wilderness Adventure, she had tried to forget about Andy, but her feelings had always lingered. Now the attraction had come back full force. And here in Paris, they were safe from danger—there were no evil counselors, no chance of drowning in whitewater rapids, and no Eric around to make her feel guilty.

Immediately she started to feel guilty. Eric wasn't here, but he was still her boyfriend, no matter where he was.

Resolutely she battled the guilt. She was *not* going to waste a beautiful day in Paris thinking about anything that might make her feel bad, or sad, or anything other than sublimely happy.

And it *was* a beautiful day. Even through the closed curtains, she could see the sunlight streaming in. She jumped out of bed, pulled back the curtains, and flung open the door that led out onto the tiny balcony. Stepping outside, she closed her eyes and let the warmth of the sun envelop her. The waves of contentment came flooding back.

Opening her eyes, she admired the street below her. Paris was such a clean city. A woman was pulling up the blinds in a cheese store, the baker was arranging loaves of bread in his shop window, and the newspaper vendor was opening his stand. Amy felt like she was watching Paris wake up. At Café Chocolat, the first customers were arriving and taking seats at the little outdoor tables. She recognized some of the regulars who were there every day—the two gray-haired men who played chess, the curly-haired woman with glasses who was always scribbling in a notebook, and—Amy blinked to make sure she was seeing properly.

What was Annie doing there?

At that moment Annie looked up and saw her. She waved and beckoned. Even from this distance, Amy could see the anxious expression on her face.

Amy nodded and held up a finger to indicate that she'd be down in a minute. Hastily she retreated back into the room, pulled on some clothes, and hurried out the door.

In the lobby, Madame Anselme was on the telephone. She waved to Amy, and Amy waved back, but she didn't stop. She raced across the street to the café. "Annie! Is everything okay?"

"That is what I came to ask you," Annie said. "I was very worried."

"About what?"

"You! You were supposed to call me last night!"

"I was?" Amy remembered Annie giving her a phone number, and she recalled saying something like "Talk to you later."

"Oh, I'm sorry, Annie. I just forgot, I guess."

Annie looked disapproving. "Then calling me must not have been very important to you."

Amy felt bad. "I would have called you today," she assured Annie.

"But you said, 'Talk to you later,' not 'Talk to you to-morrow.' Or perhaps I did not understand your English."

"No, that's what I said," Amy told her. She didn't know how to explain it any better. Maybe French people took something as casual as "Talk to you later" more seriously than Americans did. "Anyway, what's up?"

"Up?" Annie looked puzzled and raised her eyes to the sky.

Amy used a French phrase that basically meant the same thing. *"Quoi de neuf?"*

Annie's expression cleared. "Oh, I see. Well, school is closed today, and I have no ballet rehearsals. So we can spend the entire day together!"

Amy hoped Annie wouldn't notice how she hesitated before smiling and responding. "Great!" She hoped she sounded sincere. She told herself that she *should* sound sincere. After all, she'd been so happy about finding

Annie. And she was still happy. But it was too bad she couldn't be alone with Andy.

"What would you like to do?" Annie asked.

"Andy's coming to meet me . . . *us*. So let's decide when he gets here."

The waiter appeared, and they gave their orders for the *petit déjeuner*. Then Monica joined them. "Madame Anselme said that your mother called this morning. At least, I *think* that's what she said. Anyway, I called back but Nancy wasn't in her hotel room. Here comes Christophe!"

Amy watched as the Frenchman sauntered toward them, and she made a silent vow. Whatever she and Annie and Andy decided to do that day, they were *not* going to include him. Anyway, he and Monica already had plans, so she didn't have to worry about it.

Or so she thought. "I have spoken to my friends," he told Monica. "They will be happy to see you at the party today. Of course, Amy is invited also. And your friend may come too."

"We're going to do something else," Amy started to say, but Annie was curious. "What kind of party is this?"

Christophe made a big show of looking around to make sure no one was listening to him. He dropped his voice to a whisper. "My friends and I are gathering in the Catacombs. There'll be music, wine, and dancing."

Amy looked at him in disbelief. "You dance around the skulls and the bones?"

Christophe laughed. "Oh, no, *ma petite*, what you speak of, that is the public section of the Catacombs. We do not go there."

Annie's eyes were wide. "Do you go through a secret entrance to a forbidden area?" she asked, turning to Amy. "Remember, the guide spoke of people who do such things."

Amy remembered. "Yes. He said it's dangerous and illegal. Monica, I don't think you should go."

Christophe made one of those sweeping hand gestures. "Nonsense. The police will not bother us on a holiday. And it is not dangerous if one knows the route."

Monica was looking at Christophe excitedly, and Amy couldn't blame her. Who would listen to a twelve-year-old when a handsome man was offering an adventure?

But there was an unexpected response from Annie. "I would like to come to this party."

"Annie!" Amy cried in dismay.

"I would like to see this secret place," Annie continued. "Amy, it will be so interesting! Please, we must have this experience together."

Amy was relieved to see Andy approaching. Maybe he could come up with an alternate plan that would intrigue Annie more than the Catacombs. He hailed them with the French version of "Hi, everyone"—*"Salut, tout le monde,"* and pulled another chair to the table.

Before Amy could even return the greeting, Annie spoke up. "We are all going to a party in the Catacombs today."

Andy stared at her. "A party in the Catacombs?" he repeated.

Amy could see that he wasn't crazy about the idea, but at least they'd be together. "It's okay if Andy comes too, right?" she asked Christophe.

"But of course! It is, how do you say in English—the more, the merrier!"

Andy was silent for a moment. Then he said, "I'd rather not go to the Catacombs."

Annie raised her eyebrows. "Have you no sense of adventure? Are you not just a little bit curious to find a secret passage into the underground tunnels?" She sounded like she was mocking him for a lack of courage.

"Not really. If I was curious, I could look for the old secret entrance just below our school."

Annie frowned. "I still believe that is simply a rumor."

The atmosphere was tense. Amy was certainly willing to consider other options besides hanging out in the Catacombs. "Do you want to do something else?" she asked Andy eagerly.

"Amy!" Annie exclaimed. "You promised you would spend this day with me! And I want to go to the party!"

Amy didn't recall giving any kind of promise. But Annie looked positively devastated, as if Amy had just broken her heart. Amy gazed at Andy beseechingly. "Please come with us, Andy."

The waiter returned and asked Andy if he wanted something. In French, Andy replied no, that he had to leave. He murmured, *"Au revoir,"* and started to go. Amy ran after him.

"Andy! Why won't you come?"

"Because it's not something that interests me. I wish you wouldn't go either. It can be dangerous."

"Annie will be so upset if I abandon her, and—" She stopped. "That's why you're not coming, isn't it? You don't like Annie."

Andy wouldn't look her straight in the eye. "Actually, I've got some other stuff to do. I'll meet you tonight, okay? *Just* you. Here at the café, seven o'clock."

She nodded. And without another word, he took off. Watching him, she knew his reasons had nothing to do with danger or other stuff to do. He just didn't want to hang out with Annie.

Amy returned to the table, and Annie smiled at her.

"Thank you for agreeing to stay with me," she said warmly. "It'll be fun."

"Yeah," Amy murmured. Her only consolation was that Andy was meeting her that evening. She had a feeling that if she'd run off with him, Annie would never have spoken to her again. She certainly didn't want that. Annie was her clone! Her sister! But why weren't she and Andy hitting it off?

Christophe's entrance was through an apartment building. He had a special code that he punched in to open the main door; then he led them through a courtyard to a trapdoor. He lifted it and started down a flight of stairs that ended in a dank, dark basement. Christophe's flashlight offered some visibility, but it was still very creepy, and Amy could have sworn she heard mice—maybe rats—scuttling about.

Annie didn't seem bothered by it, though. And Monica was giggling nervously. "I hope you know where you're going, Christophe," she said.

Apparently he did. He opened a heavy metal door, and they followed him into a tunnel. It was narrow, so they walked in single file, without saying much for a while. Then Amy's sensitive ears picked up a sound, off in the distance. It was music and it sounded like the girl group TLC.

It was. Christophe turned abruptly, and there, in a

cavernous gallery dimly illuminated by a lantern, half a dozen people sat around while strains of music poured out of a boom box.

Christophe and his friends greeted each other, and he proceeded to introduce his entourage.

There were four other young men and two women. The guys all had longish hair, like Christophe's, but they weren't as good-looking. In fact, they looked pretty grungy. One of them was wearing sunglasses, which was ridiculous since no ray of sun was ever going to hit this place. The girls both had heavy black makeup that practically obliterated their eyes, and one of them was smoking.

Some blankets were spread on the wet ground, and Amy saw sandwiches and a bottle of wine scattered there. The thought of eating in this nasty environment wasn't the least bit appealing. The blankets didn't look much cleaner than the floor of the cavern. And the walls were covered with graffiti, an abstract painting, and in very large white letters, someone had written LE CHÂTEAU on the wall. The castle. As if.

Monica looked dazed and intrigued. Annie was already deep in conversation with one of Christophe's friends, asking him questions about the Catacombs. Amy tried to strike up a dialogue with the nonsmoking girl. In French, she asked if the girl was an artist.

The girl stared at her coldly. "We are all artists. Only true artists can appreciate the beauty here."

"I guess I'm not an artist, then," Amy said. The girl looked at her icily and turned away.

Two more of Christophe's friends lit up cigarettes, and suddenly Amy craved fresh air. She wasn't going to find much down here, but maybe she could at least get away from the tobacco smell.

She edged around the group to the arch where they'd entered. The tunnel wasn't any more inviting than the gallery, but she thought there might be more gallery spaces up ahead. She slipped out and took a few steps in the tunnel.

Her extraordinary vision enabled her to see in the pitch darkness. After walking a few minutes, she came to a junction, where the tunnel split into two directions. Neither of these paths looked like they'd ever been taken.

"Eeny, meeny, miney, mo," she whispered to herself, and went to the left. After a while, the ceiling dropped, and she had to bow her head. Then it dropped even more. If she wanted to go any farther, she'd have to get down on her hands and knees.

The thought made her shudder. She decided to head back to the smoke-filled party. Maybe by now Annie was bored and ready to leave.

Then her ears perked up. There was a noise, coming from ahead. She concentrated. It didn't sound like any kind of nasty rodent.

She made out voices, but she couldn't hear what they were saying.

Without giving herself time to change her mind, she dropped to her hands and knees and crawled on. As she got closer, she realized she was hearing a voice speak English, but with a heavy accent. There was no music, but it was probably just another party. She would never have guessed there was so much social life going on under the streets of Paris. And if this party was like the one she'd left, the guests probably wouldn't appreciate any party crashers.

Amy was about to start crawling backward when she picked up some understandable words. The man's voice was guttural.

"They must be destroyed. All of them. Filthy, disgusting vermin. They are a blight on the face of the earth."

Despite the thick accent, the hostility in his tone came across loud and clear. Amy wondered what he could be talking about. Rats, maybe? She herself had some pretty hostile feelings toward rodents. But this guy sounded really angry.

A woman's voice responded. She had a different accent than the man, but she sounded equally disturbed. "I'll tell you the ones I truly despise. The ones who come from Asia."

Asian rats? Was that a larger-than-usual species?

The man spoke. "Yes, they are as reprehensible as the Africans. Only a different color."

"But not white." That was a new voice, another man.

"No, certainly not white," the woman agreed. "But there are also many white ones who must be eradicated."

"Yes, of course," a third man said. "Like the ones who do not have full use of their arms and legs."

"They are weak," the first man acknowledged. "Those wheelchairs take up too much space."

Rats in wheelchairs? Then Amy shuddered.

They weren't talking about rats. They were talking about *people*.

twelve

Slowly, silently, Amy crawled forward. She could see a little light now, coming from the right side of the tunnel. Above her the ceiling had risen, and she could have stood up, but something told her to stay low.

Some distance ahead, she could see an arch that led to a gallery. A large group was gathered inside. Each person wore a black armband with a crooked white cross on it.

Amy was familiar with the symbol from her history textbook. It was the symbol of the German Nazi party in World War II. A swastika.

"*Arrêtez!*" a voice behind her said sharply. "Stop!"

Amy leaped up and turned, expecting to see a police officer. But it wasn't.

It was Sébastien, the guide who had led them on the tour of the public Catacombs.

"You should not be here," he scolded her.

"I know, I know," she said quickly. "I'm sorry." She remembered her encounter with the police in the subway and tried the same tactic. "I'm just a stupid tourist." She frowned. "What are *you* doing here?"

"I give tours of the Catacombs," Sébastien said curtly. "And I also patrol the tunnels."

"Then you know about the people in that gallery over there, don't you? Something very creepy is going on! They're full of hate. They want to destroy everyone who isn't like them."

"I will take care of this. It is nothing for you to think about. Now please follow me."

"No thanks, I know my own way out," Amy said quickly. She scurried past Sébastien, hoping he wouldn't notice how rapidly she moved in the darkness. She wanted to get away.

She was extremely grateful for her powerful sense of direction. A normal person could easily have gotten completely lost. But she found her way back to Christophe's gallery—just in time to see two real uniformed police officers escorting them all out.

Amy gulped. Were they all going to be arrested now? She hesitated. But staying down here certainly wasn't an option, especially with those crazy people in the other gallery. So she joined the group and listened to the police officers' stern lecture as they led them out the way they'd come in.

But they weren't arrested. "This entrance will be sealed today," one policeman told them. "Do not attempt to find another way into the Catacombs. Unless, of course, you wish to encounter the fate of Philibert Aspairt."

Amy recalled the story of the man who had gotten lost in the Catacombs, not to be found for eleven years. She definitely didn't want to end her days like him. In fact, now that she'd seen the Catacombs twice, she was perfectly content never to see them again.

The police, however, went back inside. Amy assumed they would continue to patrol the tunnels, and she hoped they'd find and arrest the Nazi group.

Christophe's friends dispersed. Christophe himself was comforting a slightly shaken-up Monica, and Amy and Annie walked together. Amy couldn't stop thinking about her experience.

"I should have told the police something."

"Told them what?"

Amy described what she had seen in the tunnels.

"Annie, it was so *foul*! Those people were wearing Nazi armbands! They were talking about destroying anyone who isn't white or completely healthy."

"I have heard that many political groups have meetings in the Catacombs," Annie said.

"This wasn't exactly political, Annie. They were Nazis! The Nazis murdered twelve million people in World War Two! Six million Jews, plus Gypsies, the handicapped, gay people—anyone they felt was inferior to them."

"Yes, yes, I know all that," Annie said, almost impatiently. "It was Nazi Germany that occupied France, remember? I do know my French history."

"Sorry." Amy remembered how annoyed Annie had been at Andy for knowing more about Paris than she did. Now Amy was doing the same thing, trying to teach Annie her own history. "But aren't you shocked, to think that there are still Nazis running around?" she asked.

Annie was philosophical about it. "There are many unusual groups of people in the world, Amy. People with different attitudes, religions, ideas. They are free to express their beliefs here in France, just as in the United States."

She was right. Amy had seen news programs about the Ku Klux Klan, a bunch of American fanatics who dressed in long white sheets and hoods and marched around proclaiming that black people were inferior to white people. The world was full of crazies. But even the dumbest maniacs had the right to express their beliefs.

As long as they didn't harm anyone.

She tried not to think about the Nazis for the rest of the day. Monica and Christophe went off by themselves, while Annie took Amy window shopping. That proved to be a good distraction for a while, but Amy couldn't completely erase the scene in the Catacombs. And she *wanted* to think about it.

At dinnertime Annie left her to go home. She invited Amy to come along, but Amy declined. She already had plans to meet Andy, which Annie clearly didn't approve of. It didn't matter. If Annie and Andy didn't like each other, Amy would just have to divide her time between them.

Andy was waiting for her at Café Chocolat at seven o'clock. The second he saw her face, he knew something was wrong.

"What's the matter? What happened?"

Despite her depression, she felt a warm tingle shoot through her. He had to care about her deeply to detect so quickly that she had things on her mind.

"I saw something really strange today," she began, and told him all about the experience in the Catacombs.

He listened intently. "Did any of the Nazis see you?"

"No . . . Oh, Andy, what should we do? I didn't even know Nazis still existed."

"They're called neo-Nazis," Andy said.

"The people I heard in the Catacombs were speaking English," Amy told him. "But they all had different accents. They were definitely from different countries."

"They're all over the place," Andy said glumly. "Even America."

"What should we do?" she asked again.

"Nothing."

She was taken aback. "Nothing? Shouldn't I go tell the police what I heard?"

Andy shook his head. "Neo-Nazis are ignorant people. Unfortunately, there will always be groups like that around. You can't take them seriously."

That was basically what Annie had said. Still, Amy couldn't take them so lightly. "But Andy," she said, "what if they start making real efforts to get what they want?"

"Don't worry so much. Those people are full of talk." Andy took Amy's hand. "Look, it's a beautiful night, we're in Paris, and we're finally alone. Let's go get something to eat."

They started down the street together. It was nice,

walking quietly like this, but there was something else troubling her that she wanted to ask him.

"Andy . . ."

"Hmm?"

"Why don't you like Annie?"

She felt his hand tighten, but this time it wasn't from affection. "Could we talk about something else?" He sounded really annoyed, and he let out a deep sigh.

"Andy, is something wrong?"

"I've just got a lot on my mind too."

"Like what?"

He was silent. Then he said, "Oh, just school stuff. A test coming up, a paper to finish, that sort of thing. I'd rather not discuss it, okay?"

Amy was bewildered. "If we can't talk about the neo-Nazis, and we can't talk about Annie, what are we allowed to talk about?"

Andy smiled. "Let's talk about dinner. Want to try some French pizza?"

thirteen

Amy opened her eyes the next morning to another beautiful day. Only this time, she didn't feel any lovely waves of contentment washing over her.

She hadn't slept well. No nightmares had kept her awake, just a general restlessness. There were too many troubling thoughts crowding her head. Like the neo-Nazis.

And Andy. She couldn't quite put her finger on it, but something was wrong, and it was all very confusing.

Their evening together had been lovely. They'd eaten a really good pizza and gone to a fair in the

Tuileries gardens by the Louvre, where they'd played a few games and taken a ride on the Ferris wheel. It had stopped while they were at the top, and Andy had pointed out some important sights. But every time Amy asked him anything personal—why he'd chosen to become an exchange student in Paris, when he planned on going back to the United States—he became vague and changed the subject. It was as if he had some secret that he couldn't share with her.

She thought maybe he was in some kind of trouble back home or here in Paris. That maybe he'd committed a crime and was in hiding. It would explain why he'd tried to hide his identity from her when she first saw him. He didn't want to get her involved. But what kind of crime could Andy have committed? Nothing made sense.

She glanced over at Monica and saw that her eyes were open. And she was smiling.

"What are you thinking about?" Amy asked her.

"Christophe."

"Oh."

Monica sat up. "Amy, I know I said I was taking a vacation from men. But Christophe is different. There's something so pure about him."

"Pure?" Amy repeated doubtfully. That wasn't a word she would ever associate with Christophe.

"Maybe because he's so carefree," Monica mused. "He hasn't been corrupted by the working world."

"No kidding," Amy murmured. She had a feeling that Christophe had never done a day of work in his life.

"He doesn't get any appreciation as an artist here," Monica continued. "The art establishment is just too conservative, he says. I'll bet he'd do very well in the U.S. if he knew the right people who could connect him."

"People like you?" Amy teased.

Monica smiled.

Amy tried to smile back, though the thought of Christophe DuPont living next door to her in Los Angeles didn't thrill her. Clearly, Monica saw something in him that Amy couldn't see. She just hoped that for once Monica was right about a guy.

At least Christophe wasn't spending the day with them. They hit more museums, Amy's favorite being the Rodin Museum, where she was transfixed by a sculpture called *The Kiss*. It showed a man and woman locked in a passionate embrace. She was glad Andy wasn't with her. It made her blush.

She was supposed to see him tonight. Amy had told him she would be coming to the Lycée Internationale to meet Annie when the school day was over, and though she knew it was hopeless, she had invited him to hang with them. But he'd said he had something to do right after school, and he'd meet her at Café Chocolat. She'd have to be satisfied with that.

At three o'clock Amy left Monica back at the Louvre Museum. She was burned out on art and took off to meet Annie.

It was still early when she reached the Lycée Internationale. School wouldn't let out for at least half an hour. As she gazed at the impressive building, she started wondering if the inside was anything like an American school.

Why not find out?

The lobby was empty when she opened the front door, and she didn't see any offices nearby. She suspected she shouldn't be doing this, but if anyone caught her she'd just go into her dumb tourist routine. She walked quickly down a hall, thinking she'd be able to get a look at classrooms through the door windows. But the doors in this school didn't have windows, so there wasn't much to see.

She went into a stairwell and was about to go upstairs when she heard voices. Not ready to get caught just yet, she went downstairs instead.

There didn't seem to be much going on down below. In fact, this lower level appeared to be totally deserted. She wandered around for a while, peeking inside closets stuffed with reams of paper, cartons of chalk, and other school supplies. Nothing very intriguing.

One door led into a much larger room, and in the darkness she could make out shelves of books. She hit a light switch on the wall. The resulting illumination came from just one weak bulb, but it was enough for her to peruse the bookcases.

This was definitely more interesting. She discovered old French textbooks, dusty and full of old-fashioned pictures and out-of-date information. One was a history of the United States published in 1955, which stated that the U.S. was made up of forty-eight states. Another was a science book published in 1962, which ended with John Glenn's orbit of the moon as the most amazing feat in space.

Most of the stuff was fascinating, but one book gave her the creeps. It was a math textbook, and the inside cover was stamped with the name of the school and the year 1942. That was during the German Occupation.

Part of the stamp bore a swastika. Seeing it sent a chill through Amy.

She almost dropped the book when she heard the door to the room open. Silently she bent down behind the bookcase. She really didn't want to have to play stupid tourist again if she didn't absolutely have to. And what would a tourist be doing in the lower level of a Paris high school anyway?

In her crouched position, she peered between some books and saw a figure moving toward the far wall. The person then proceeded to pull a packed bookcase away from the wall without much effort. That seemed really odd. Rising slightly, Amy found another gap between two books to look through.

It was a good thing that the bookcase made a loud scraping sound, because it masked Amy's sharp intake of breath. The person pulling the bookcase was Andy.

What was he up to?

Finally the wall behind the bookcase was exposed. The only thing she could see was a long crack running down part of the wall. She watched as Andy placed his fingers on the crack—no, *in* the crack. In fact, it wasn't a crack, it was the edge of a door.

Suddenly Amy remembered that Andy had said there

was an old entrance to the Catacombs under the school. This had to be it.

He got the door slightly open, just wide enough for him to slip through. As he did, he turned slightly, and that was when she saw it.

A black armband. On Andy's right arm.

With the mark of a swastika.

fourteen

So that was the secret. That was what he was hiding from her. He was one of *them*.

Long after he had disappeared through the hidden door in the wall, Amy remained frozen behind the bookcase.

Andy . . . her Andy was a Nazi. A neo-Nazi. As if there was any real difference.

Suddenly she felt faint. She rushed out of the book room and found a rest room down the hall. She splashed water on her face and looked at her reflection in the mirror. Was it the lighting, or had her complexion gone completely white?

Unanswerable questions filled her head. How could this be happening? How could someone like Andy—someone kind, and thoughtful, and caring—be part of a neo-Nazi group? How could she have been so wrong about him? Maybe he wasn't Andy Decker after all, but another, *bad* Andy. She had met an Amy who was evil; certainly it was possible that there were evil Andys running around too.

But she knew that the Andy here in Paris was the same Andy she'd known at Wilderness Adventure. She had *felt* it.

His actions in the book room suddenly explained why he hadn't gone with them into the Catacombs, she thought bitterly. He'd been afraid he might run into some of his fellow Nazis and they'd give him away.

The door of the rest room opened, and a woman spoke to her in French. She wanted to know who Amy was and what she was doing there. Amy brushed past her, mumbling something about being a stupid tourist. For once, she was telling the absolute truth. She was a tourist. And she had to be stupid, to have cared for a guy like Andy.

Outside the school, she moved toward the street in a daze and didn't even hear Annie calling out. It wasn't until Annie grabbed her by the arm that Amy stopped walking.

"Amy, where have you been? It is a very poor habit to be late all the time!" Annie cut short her rebuke when she got a good look at Amy's face. Immediately her tone changed. "Amy! Is something wrong?"

"Yes," Amy said. "Something is very wrong." Then, in the midst of students and passersby, she burst into tears.

Annie was startled. She hustled Amy across the street and through the gates of the Luxembourg Gardens. "Now, tell me what has happened," she ordered Amy as she sat them down on a bench.

"It's Andy," Amy sobbed. "You see, he's one of *us*. And he's one of *them*."

Annie frowned. "Amy, perhaps my English is not so good, but I do not understand what you are saying."

Amy abandoned any concern about protecting Andy's privacy. She poured out the whole story, about how Andy was a product of another clone project, and how he was mixed up with the neo-Nazis in the Catacombs. She finished off with the report of what she'd just witnessed in the basement of the Lycée Internationale.

"I never liked that boy," Annie said flatly when Amy stopped talking. "I could not understand your friendship with him. He is not to be trusted. I have suspected this."

"Really?" Amy asked. "But you only just met him."

"I have very instinctive feelings about people," Annie replied. "You are like me, surely you also have these immediate reactions to people."

Annie was right. Unfortunately for Amy, however, sometimes her instinctive feelings turned out to be wrong.

"But I am not being kind," Annie went on. "I see that you felt strongly for him." She shook her head sadly. "Men can be so deceptive. My mother has always told me this."

Amy was momentarily distracted from her own woes by this comment. It was the first time Annie had ever really mentioned a parent. "What are your mother and father like?"

"Oh, they are very fine people," Annie assured her. "They come from the families of French aristocracy. An ancestor of my father was a duke, and my mother's family is descended from the last king of France."

That was certainly impressive. "Do you get along with them?"

"Yes," Annie said. "When they adopted me, they were quite concerned about what sort of blood I came from. So when they learned of my exceptional background, they were quite pleased."

Amy wasn't sure how to take this. She couldn't

imagine her own mother caring about what kind of blood her adopted child had, as long as it was healthy blood.

Thinking about her mother made her suddenly long to talk to her. She looked at her watch. Nancy would be back in the hotel room now, changing for dinner.

Amy looked around. "Do you see a telephone anywhere?"

"Who do you want to call?"

"My mother. I'm kind of missing her right now."

"You should not bother her with your problems," Annie said. "She will be unhappy and perhaps leave her conference."

Annie had a point. Her mother had been very excited about this conference, and she didn't want to ruin it for her.

Annie continued. "Your mother might decide to take you back to America immediately. Then who knows when we will see each other again?"

"You're right." Amy stood up. "I've been deceived by a terrible guy, and this happens to girls all the time. I'll just have to get over it."

Annie nodded with approval. "Precisely. I will help you to get over it. Tonight we will go to a special gathering. A kind of party. It will help you understand me better. But first I think you should change your clothes. You are very dirty."

As Amy looked down at her top and jeans, she realized the dust from the old textbooks had gotten all over her. She didn't feel much like a party, but she did need to change.

They walked back to the hotel, and Amy glanced across the street to see if Monica was sitting at Café Chocolat. She wasn't—but Christophe was there, talking on his mobile phone.

Amy couldn't hear him over the noise of the street, but she saw his mouth form the name *Monica*. "Can you read lips?" she asked Annie.

"You mean, in the habit of deaf people?" Annie seemed taken aback. "No, I have no deaf friends."

"I learned how to do it in a school program," Amy told her. She was still watching Christophe. Something about his smile really bugged her. "I'm going to read his lips and repeat what he's saying," she said. "So if I don't understand everything you can translate for me."

Annie shrugged. "All right."

Speaking softly, Amy followed the movement of Christophe's lips and relayed the words. *"Je crois qu'elle est riche. Ou, peut-être, que l'enfant est riche. Je ne sais pas qui, mais quelqu'un l'est, et j'ai besoin d'argent."*

Her French was getting so good, Amy knew what

132

Christophe was saying even before Annie translated. "I think she's rich. Or maybe the child is rich. I don't know who, but someone is, and I need money."

"I knew it," Amy said. "He doesn't care about Monica at all."

"I fear not," Annie agreed. "He is truly a gigolo, I think. He is only interested in her money."

"Another deceptive man," Amy declared grimly. "Just like Andy. Poor Monica. She's picked herself another loser." She turned to Annie. "Let's do something." If she couldn't get her revenge on Andy for turning out to be a liar, she was all too glad to take her anger out on *this* creep.

"Look, there is Monica now," Annie pointed out. They watched as Monica joined Christophe at the café. Christophe immediately ended his phone call. "Can Monica speak or understand French?"

"Not a word," Amy said.

"Then I have an idea. It will make Christophe go away without causing Monica a terrible heartbreak." She shared her plan with Amy, and Amy approved. Together they walked across the street to the café.

When she saw them coming, Monica waved happily. Christophe greeted them with a smile. "Ah, all my lovely ladies are here! Have you made plans for the evening?"

With a very sweet smile of her own, Annie answered

him in rapid French. From her expression, anyone who didn't know the language would have thought she was saying something incredibly nice. But with a little concentration, Amy understood everything she said.

"We're on to what you're up to. You think Monica is a rich American or that Amy might be. And that you can get money from them. Maybe you think you can seduce Monica or kidnap Amy, but if you're smart, you'll excuse yourself with a good reason right this minute, or I will go to the police."

Amy had to admit that Christophe was a good actor. His smile didn't waver for one second. When Annie stopped, he spoke smoothly in English.

"I very much wish I could join you this evening, but I fear it is impossible. You see, I have been invited to display my art at an exhibition in the south of France. I must leave Paris immediately."

"For how long?" Monica asked in dismay.

"I will be away for at least one week."

"But that means I won't see you again! We're going back to California in a few days!"

"Nonsense, *chérie*. When there is true love, it conquers all distance. If I sell my paintings, I will use the money to come to California. Until then . . ." He took her hand and kissed the back of it. *"Au revoir, mon amour."* He turned to Amy and Annie. "And to you girls . . ." He said something in French that Amy couldn't understand at all.

Then he was gone.

"What did he say?" Amy asked Annie in a whisper.

"It was a slang expression," Annie whispered back. "One that nice people never use."

Poor Monica looked stricken. Amy was sorry for her, but she knew Monica would feel worse if she knew the truth about Christophe. She put her hand on Monica's and squeezed it. "Let's do something nice tonight. Anything you want."

"I have a suggestion," Annie said. "I wanted to take Amy to a party this evening. Let me bring you both."

Monica smiled sadly. "That's very sweet, Annie, but I don't think I want to go to a party for teenagers."

"Oh, the party will have many adults," Annie said.

Monica sighed. "I suppose it won't do me any good to sit around and mope. Do you want to go to the party, Amy?"

Amy really didn't. But she knew Monica wouldn't leave her alone at the hotel. And if a party would make Monica feel better, she'd go along.

"Okay," she said. "Let's party."

fteen

When Annie returned to the hotel that evening, she looked very chic in a tight, short black skirt and jersey top, with a jaunty red-and-black scarf tied around her neck.

"Do I look okay?" Amy asked doubtfully. She suddenly felt like she might look a little babyish in her flowered skirt and pink twinset.

"You are perfect," Annie assured her. And she was equally nice about the way Monica was dressed—in a vintage 1970s disco outfit, with huge bell-bottom pants and a glitter top. Amy was relieved. With Annie's tendency to poke fun at people who looked different, Amy had been afraid she'd find Monica's look embarrassing.

"Where is the party?" Monica asked as they went out into the Paris night.

"It is a little far from here," Annie said. "We will take the Métro."

They walked in silence toward the entrance to the Métro. Monica strolled slowly, lagging behind them. She was still looking a little depressed. Amy didn't feel much like talking either.

In a whisper so soft only another clone could hear her, Annie asked, "Are you still thinking about Andy?"

"A little," Amy admitted. "Actually, a lot."

Annie didn't scold her. "You will feel better soon."

Amy tried to pull herself together. Annie was being incredibly nice.

"There's something I've been meaning to ask you," Amy said. "All the original Project Crescent girls were called Amy. I was Amy, Number Seven. What was your number?"

"I do not know," Annie said. "My parents told me that my original name was Amy, but of course, they changed it."

"Why?"

"Because Amy sounds like *ami*, which means 'friend' in French," Annie explained. "It is not suitable as a first name."

"It's a nice word, though," Amy commented.

"Yes," Annie said, smiling. "Even though my name is not Amy, I am always your *amie*."

That was really sweet, Amy thought. Andy had turned out to be a despicable Nazi, but at least Annie was proving herself to be a true friend. It cheered her up a little.

They rode the Métro for a while, and then Annie indicated it was time to get off. "We have to change to a different train here," she told them.

This station was much bigger than any of the others Amy had been in so far. She was totally confused by all the possible directions to go in, and all the signs and arrows meant nothing to her. But Annie took charge.

"Eight different lines run through this station," she told them. "Including trains that go out to the suburbs."

There were certainly a lot of people around, and the three of them were constantly getting separated. "Keep your eyes on me," Annie warned them. "It's easy to get lost here."

Amy had no intention of getting lost, and she held on to one of the tassels that hung from Monica's blouse so she wouldn't get lost either. It was funny, in a way—her mother had wanted Monica to come so she could chaperone Amy, but Amy felt like *she* was the one watching out for her baby-sitter.

The crowd thinned a little as Annie led them from one twisting corridor to another. Since Annie knew where she was going, Amy didn't pay attention to the signs, but Monica noticed one.

"What does *interdit* mean?"

Amy knew the answer. "It means 'forbidden.' Why?"

"That's what the last sign said."

Amy suddenly realized that they were the only people in this corridor. "Uh-oh. Annie, I think we took a wrong turn."

"No, we didn't," Annie said. "I have done this before. It is a shortcut to the other platform."

Some shortcut. It seemed like they'd been wandering for ages. "We go down here," Annie said, and made a sudden turn to the right. "It is a good shortcut, yes? No more crowds."

There certainly weren't any crowds. In fact, there didn't seem to be a soul in sight. As the three of them went down another flight of stairs, Amy could hear the echo of their footsteps.

At the bottom of the steps, Annie turned. The lighting was getting very dim. With the next turn, it grew even dimmer. Finally Annie said, "We're almost there," and she motioned them to the left. But then they all stopped.

"Annie, this can't be right," Monica said. "There's no light down here."

"I don't know what—"

But they weren't going to find out what Annie didn't know. From out of the pitch darkness, the figures of a man and a woman appeared. "You will come with us," the woman said.

Amy squinted. "Who are you?" she asked.

The woman didn't answer, but she didn't need to. Amy could now see the black armbands that both she and the man were wearing. "Ohmigod, we're in the Catacombs," she said.

"You will come with us," the woman repeated.

"No, I don't think so," Amy said coldly. "Come on, you guys. Let's get out of here." But the man grabbed her arm.

"Hey, what do you think you're doing?" Monica cried in outrage.

"Don't touch her!" Annie shouted.

The man was very strong. And although Amy had

greater physical strength than any normal twelve-year-old girl, she had to struggle to free herself from this big man's grip. She could hear Annie gasp, and Monica let out a shriek as Amy went into a martial arts stance and kicked the man in the head. He staggered backward. The woman moved toward Annie, but she wasn't very big, and Amy knew Annie could handle her.

She couldn't give the man a chance to recover. Grabbing Monica's hand, she took off. Monica was shrieking all the way down the corridor, and she continued to wail as Amy dragged her around a corner. Amy wasn't sure if this was the way they'd come, but she figured Annie would let out a yell if Amy made a wrong turn. She hoped Annie could run in that tight skirt.

She saw some steps and ran toward them. At the same time, a man appeared out of the shadows.

Amy stopped short as she realized she was once again face-to-face with Sébastien, the guide to the Catacombs.

"You again!" he exclaimed angrily.

"We got lost," Amy said, expecting Annie to start explaining what happened. But Annie wasn't with them.

"Ohmigod, they got Annie!" Monica cried out.

"What are you talking about?" Sébastien demanded.

Amy's voice shook; she tried to get the words out as fast as she could. "There was another girl with us, Annie Perrault. She took the tour of the Catacombs with me. We look alike. Those neo-Nazis tried to grab us, and we started running. I thought Annie was right behind us."

Sébastien didn't look concerned. "I'm sure your friend will be fine."

"But I'm telling you that neo-Nazis took her. They're awful people."

Sébastien still didn't look anxious, just terribly annoyed. "I am taking you two out of here right now, and I never want to see you near the Catacombs again."

"We're not leaving without Annie," Amy declared.

Just then they heard the sound of footsteps coming down the stairs. Two uniformed police officers appeared.

"What's happening here?" one asked in French.

Sébastien reached into his pocket and produced an official-looking card. Amy figured the card had to do with his job as a guide. "Please take these women out," he told the police. To Amy he said, "I will locate your friend."

Amy tried to protest, but the police took her and Monica's arms and led them out. They had no opportunity to go into a dumb tourist routine. The officers put them in a van and told them they were being taken to the police station on charges of trespassing.

Monica couldn't understand them, but she figured out what was happening and started to wail. Amy tried to calm her down at the same time that she tried to reason with the officers. "But my friend, *mon amie*, she's down there," Amy shouted. "Please let us go."

The police closed the van door in her face.

sixteen 16

Amy lay on her bed in the hotel room and stared at a crack in the ceiling. She turned to look at Monica, snoring softly in the other bed. How could she sleep after the evening they'd just had?

They had both been totally freaked to find themselves being taken to a police station. Amy didn't know which possibility was scarier—going to jail, or her mother's reaction when she got a call saying her daughter was under arrest. And maybe worse things were in store for them.

It turned out that the waiting was worse than the actual experience. Since Monica didn't speak any French, they had to sit for over an hour with some unsavory people while a bilingual police officer was located. In her disco outfit, Monica fit right in.

Finally a policewoman appeared. After a short but stern lecture about trespassing, she let them go.

Immediately Amy wanted to go back to the Catacombs and search for Annie. But Monica refused. She was finally in baby-sitter mode and insisted that the police or Sébastien could handle the situation. She and Amy were going directly back to the hotel.

So here they were. But where was Annie? Amy had tried calling her at home, but no one had answered. She wished she could believe that Sébastien had rescued Annie from the neo-Nazis, but she didn't. There was something about him that kept her from feeling confident. He hadn't acted at all concerned when Amy first saw the neo-Nazis in the Catacombs. So maybe he wouldn't knock himself out to find Annie.

Then a chill shot up her spine as she considered a horrifying possibility.

The Nazis who came to power in Germany in the 1930s had wanted to establish a so-called master race. They believed that people who weren't just like them polluted the human race, and that if they destroyed those people, their blood would remain pure. The neo-Nazis in the Catacombs were in pursuit of the same goal. And if they learned about genetically engineered cloning experiments, wouldn't they be able to further that goal?

It was possible—more than possible; it was totally believable. It made complete sense. And how would they have found out about the existence of perfectly designed clones? Andy. Not only was Amy starting to think he was willing to sell his own soul to these people, but he was willing to betray Amy and Annie, too. How could she have been so wrong about a person?

Her eyes started to tear up. She wiped them and focused on channeling her sorrow into anger. She couldn't stay in bed any longer.

Keeping an eye on Monica, she dressed in jeans, a sweater, and sneakers, and closed the door behind her.

But she didn't make it down to the lobby. From the top of the stairs on the first landing, she saw that Madame Anselme was in her usual place behind the reception desk.

The woman didn't speak English, and she didn't know that Nancy Candler had asked her to keep an eye on Amy, but she wasn't stupid either. She was bound to wonder why a twelve-year-old girl was sneaking out of the hotel alone at midnight.

Amy crept back up the stairs and considered the options. There was one other way to get out of the hotel.

It was risky, but it was the only alternative. Holding her breath, she turned the doorknob to her room very slowly. Monica didn't stir as she went through the room and slipped out onto the balcony.

The distance to the ground wasn't that great. If she did it in two jumps—one jump to the balcony below theirs, and another jump from that balcony to the ground—she'd land safely.

Amy climbed onto the ledge. The street was deserted. She let herself drop to the lower balcony. A shriek came from inside the room.

"George! Someone's on our balcony!"

Moving faster, Amy leaped over that ledge to the ground and took off. But where was she running? She hadn't been paying that much attention when they set off for the party with Annie. And anyway, if she remembered correctly, the Métro shut down at midnight.

But there were other entrances into the Catacombs. And one of them was under the Lycée Internationale. The school would be closed, but Amy had managed to get herself into locked places before.

She ran at top speed through the streets until she reached the school, then walked around to the back. The nice thing about these old buildings was that they had lots of ornate carvings around the windows—

carvings that provided nice little niches for her to grab on to as she climbed to a window. And the window wasn't locked. It was almost *too* easy.

Once inside the building, she didn't dare turn on any lights. She relied on her extraordinary vision to find her way back down to the basement. The door to the old book room wasn't locked.

The bookcase that covered the door to the Catacombs was back in place.

She knew that moving it would require more effort than it had taken Andy, but if he could do it, so could she. And she did.

Then she used her fingertips to pry open the hidden door. When she managed to get it open wide enough to slip inside, she hesitated for the first time. It was so dark in there, and she had no idea what she would be walking into. Even with her superior eyesight, she couldn't deny the fear that was coming over her. And she couldn't completely shake it off. But she lectured herself as sternly as the policewoman had.

Your genetic sister is in trouble. And there's a boy in there who should be in trouble. Not to mention the fact that there's a disgusting gang of idiots who should be locked up.

Talking to herself always helped get her revved up. Squaring her shoulders, she entered the tunnel.

This tunnel was extremely narrow, and Amy sucked

in her breath to pass through it. She groped with her hands on both sides to feel the twists and turns and keep herself from smashing into the walls. At least she didn't hear any creepy, crawly things scuttling about. The silence was so total, it was almost like a noise. But she could hear her heart beating, and it sounded like a drum.

The ceiling dropped, and she lowered her head. It wasn't long before she had to get down on her hands and knees. The ground was moist, and tiny stones—or were they bone fragments?— pressed into the palms of her hands. She gritted her teeth and kept crawling.

Then she realized the ceiling had risen. After a few more yards, she was able to stand up again. The walls were farther apart now, and soon she couldn't touch both sides at the same time. Her eyes had adjusted somewhat to the pitch darkness, and she could see, though not too far ahead. She kept on moving. She knew there were miles of tunnels in the Catacombs. But there were many entrances, too, and this was the one she'd seen Andy enter. It had to be near the meeting place of the neo-Nazis.

Suddenly she was aware of a different sound. Footsteps . . . they were in the distance, ahead of her. But they were coming closer. And they were coming fast. Someone was running toward her.

Frantically she looked around. There was no place to hide. Then she remembered something she'd seen on her tour of the Catacombs.

She looked up. Stalactites hung like icicles from the roof of the tunnel. As the running footsteps came dangerously close, Amy leaped and grabbed on to two of them. Pulling herself up, she draped her legs around more stalactites and hoped she could hold on. It was so cold. The ice seemed to penetrate every pore in her body. Hopefully, she wouldn't have to hang there much longer. Whoever was running her way was getting very close.

She half expected to see Andy, and she imagined herself waiting until he was directly below her and then dropping down on him. The element of surprise would make him momentarily weaker than she was, and she could—

She didn't have to make that decision. It wasn't Andy. It was Sébastien again.

Amy was surprised. That guy was turning up everywhere.

At least he didn't look up. He ran under her, and she assumed he was going to the door she had come through. What if she hadn't moved the bookcase to get in? An ordinary man like Sébastien wouldn't have the strength to push it aside.

But she wasn't going to worry about Sébastien. As soon as she could no longer hear his footsteps, she let go of the stalactites and dropped down. Moving along, she became aware of a light just ahead. She listened, but she couldn't hear anyone. Even so, she slowed down and walked very carefully, ready to jump up and grab stalactites again.

She turned toward the light. No one appeared to be in that length of the tunnel, but someone had been there before. There was graffiti on the wall—a swastika and a small star, with the words YOU ARE HERE and a diagram showing various tunnels that led to a spot marked HQ. It was a map. HQ had to stand for headquarters. How kind of them to provide her with instructions.

It wasn't hard after that. Amy took a right, then a left, and then she started to hear voices. Staying as close to the wall as possible, she followed the sounds.

The voices rose. People seemed to be arguing.

"She's vital to our plans!" a man declared.

"No, not necessarily. We've got what we need."

She shrank against the wall. It was Andy's voice.

"But we'd be foolish to pass up this opportunity! It's a gift!"

A woman chimed in. "It could put us ahead of schedule! With those jeans, we'd be in a much more advanced situation."

Jeans? Amy wondered. Then it clicked. Not jeans. *Genes.*

"You've got a good point," Andy said. "I'll go after her."

"I'll go with you," the man said.

"No, let me go alone. She trusts me."

She heard him then, moving away from the people he was talking to. His footsteps became fainter.

Amy closed her eyes and fought back the tears. He was looking for *her;* he was going to lure her into coming with him so she too could be trapped down here, like Annie. How *could* he? Too bad the guillotine was no longer in use.

She couldn't spend time plotting revenge. She had to find Annie and get them both out of there. She saw that she would reach the opening to another gallery just before getting to the headquarters. If it was unoccupied, she could hide in there and listen to the people through the wall. Maybe they'd say something that would tell her where Annie was.

She edged along to the opening and peeked in. The gallery was occupied. And the occupant was Annie.

Amy rushed inside. "Annie! Are you okay?"

Annie was sitting at a desk, reading. She looked up and smiled. "Amy! I knew you'd come! I'm fine."

Amy looked back over her shoulder. "Shhh, keep your voice down. I think we can get out of here through the school door." She went back to the opening and listened. The people in the headquarters were still deep in talk. She beckoned to Annie.

"Come on, let's make a run for it."

Annie didn't move.

"Annie, come *on*!"

Annie shook her head. "No, Amy, I'm staying here."

It took Amy a minute to grasp what Annie was saying. "Annie, no! You're not one of them, are you? You can't be!"

"I am, Amy. This is where I belong."

Amy shook her head "I don't believe you! They're making you say this. Someone's threatened you!"

"Do not be ridiculous, Amy." Annie spoke calmly, as if trying to reason with a child. "I am here because I want to be here. As I said, I belong here. So do you."

Amy was aghast. "No!" She turned to flee. But she didn't get far. Someone appeared at the opening. And before she could even register that fact, a moist rag was pressed onto her face.

seventeen

Amy woke up with a headache. This wasn't a common experience for her. She rarely had any type of ache or pain. But then, she was very rarely put to sleep by artificial methods.

The sickly sweet, moist smell of the rag that had been pressed to her face still lingered. Whatever the stuff was, it had to have been pretty strong. Amy had never been knocked out before, but she suspected that someone with her highly refined genetic structure would require a more powerful dose than a normal human being. How had they known this? Had Andy told them? Had Annie?

Annie could have warned them. As her mind began to clear and her headache faded, Amy remembered everything. Annie was one of them.

She looked around. She was in another gallery, a very small one. A cell. The opening was crisscrossed with bars. Once, she had been able to bend the bars on a barricaded window to get into a building. She got up and pressed against these bars. They didn't give at all. The chloroform must have weakened her.

Her hand went automatically to the pendant around her neck, and she rubbed the crescent moon. She needed what little strength could come from remembering what she was. It didn't give her much confidence, though. After all, two other clones were now her mortal enemies.

An enormous sadness almost overwhelmed her. Andy, Annie . . . She felt so betrayed. Was there no one in the world she could trust?

"Amy, do you feel well?"

She looked up to see Annie standing just outside the bars. The French girl was actually smiling. "I know you are feeling very confused," she said. "I will try to explain it all to you." She motioned to someone outside the cell. The man who had attacked them in the Catacombs came forward and unlocked the gate. Amy considered making a run for freedom, but she knew Annie would be able to stop her. And Amy needed to conserve her strength.

Annie came in and sat down on the mat. Amy resisted an urge to slap her face. "How could you do this to me?" she asked.

"It is for your own good," Annie replied. "It is for the good of the human race. I was hoping that in time you would understand."

"Oh, I understand," Amy replied. "You're part of the organization."

"The organization that created Project Crescent? No. They were more limited in their goals. We have much higher ambitions. We are not going to cultivate genes and wait years for the beings to become useful adults. We're creating perfection within the existing human race of healthy white people."

"You're nuts," Amy declared. "You and all your Nazi pals are crazy."

Annie wasn't offended by the accusation. "I am not crazy, Amy. I am as intelligent as you are. If you will listen to me, perhaps you will understand."

Amy sincerely doubted that, but she didn't argue. The more she knew about these people, the better she'd be able to battle them.

"The world is a mess, Amy. And why is the world a mess? Because people are weak, stupid, and inferior. There is no hope for the future if these people continue to reproduce. We are going to change all that."

"How?" Amy asked.

"First we must create an army of people who can destroy everyone who is undesirable. This is what we are doing here in the Catacombs. We are experimenting with artificial growth accelerators, and steroid chemicals, and medications which sharpen the mental process. We will become smarter and stronger, until we reach the level when our intelligence and our physical power exceed so-called normal levels."

"Then what?"

Annie looked at her reprovingly. "Amy, that is a foolish question coming from you. You know what will happen. We will take over the world."

Amy knew this had to be the goal. Even so, hearing it declared so openly was appalling. She couldn't speak.

Annie went on. "Think of all the losers we see every day, Amy. It would be a better world if they didn't exist."

Amy found her voice. "But they have a *right* to exist. Just because you and I are perfect doesn't give us more of a right to exist than they have."

"Of course it does! We are what everyone should be! Think of how wonderful a world without losers, without—how do you call them in English?—creeps, nerds, wimps, dorks—would be. If there were only perfect people like us!" Her eyes became dreamy. "Surely you have felt this way. All my life I knew I was better than other people. I was so frustrated being superior and not having other people of my caliber around me. I had no one to respect, no one to look up to."

"What about your parents?" Amy asked.

"They are better than most human beings," Annie replied. "But they are not perfect. When I encountered this group down here, I felt as if I had found my true family. People who aspire to perfection. And because of my genetic perfection, I have much to contribute to their goal. So will you!" She smiled. "Amy, we are the ideal!"

"I guess Andy contributes a lot too," Amy commented, trying very hard not to show the contempt she was feeling.

Annie's smile faded. "Andy. I have doubts about him."

"What do you mean? You don't think he's a real clone?"

"He is too ambitious. He wants to do everything his

way. When you found us both here, in Paris, he wanted to take control. That is why he told you about the secret entrance, under the Lycée Internationale. He hoped you would be curious. He wanted to take the credit for bringing you into our group." She smiled smugly. "But I beat him. I am the one who will be honored for bringing you into our family."

Amy rolled her eyes. "Do you get some kind of prize?"

"Do not be sarcastic, Amy," Annie scolded. She got up. "You must rest now. You are still weak from the fumes. That is why you cannot appreciate what I am telling you. I will return later."

The man outside the gallery opened the gate and let Annie out. Amy curled up on the mat and tried to process the information she'd just been given.

This group was insane. Their goal was immoral. Her only comfort was that she doubted they had the brains to pull off their plans. Not today, at least.

But with people like Annie and Andy involved, eventually they would figure out ways to increase their own intelligence. They might learn how to do some kind of genetic transfer, extract chromosomes, synthesize DNA. The possibilities were there. And if they developed a way to replicate the genetic structure of Annie and Andy within their own existing bodies, they could become a powerful army. They could be masters of the universe, the strongest and smartest people in the world.

But they hadn't achieved that level yet.

The man guarding the entrance . . . Amy had over-powered him in the Catacombs. But not through metal bars. Now that he knew her strength, he probably wouldn't come any closer.

Unless he thought she didn't have that strength now. He must have heard Annie say that Amy was weak.

"Help," she said feebly.

The man looked through the bars. "What do you want?"

"I'm getting stiff. There's a cramp in my leg."

"Then stand up."

"I can't."

"Why not?"

"Because there's a cramp in my leg! I need help." She pressed her hands on the ground, as if to push herself up. Then she moaned, as if the mere effort had exhausted her. "I can't move! Please, help me."

The man had a long way to go before achieving perfection in intelligence. He unlocked the gate and came in. Amy lay completely still until he bent down to take her arm.

In a flash, her fist shot out. She got him right between the eyes. He fell back with a cry, but he was on his feet fairly quickly. Still, those few seconds were all Amy needed to get up and into position. A spin to give herself momentum, a kick to the head in just the right place—and he was out.

She leaped over his body and ran. But his cry had been heard, and two guys suddenly appeared, blocking the tunnel. She whirled around and took off in the opposite direction. They were chasing her, but they had a long way to go before reaching physical perfection. She could hear them panting as they tried to catch up.

She had no idea where she was going. This wasn't the way she had come in, and she didn't know where to find a way out. Then something just ahead gave her a clue.

A bone. It looked like a human arm bone, lying on the ground by a junction in the tunnel. She couldn't be far from the public part of the Catacombs.

She turned at the junction. Yes! She could see them now, the walls lined with bones and skulls.

Then she heard more voices, and running footsteps, coming from someplace ahead as well as behind her. She looked up for stalactites.

Only there weren't any stalactites in this corridor. Still, there was another way of getting herself up to the ceiling.

She started climbing the bones. The dampness in the tunnel had made them slippery, though, and it was hard for her feet to grip them. She kept sliding off.

Stretching as far as possible, she was finally able to reach the skulls that were resting on the wall of bones. She managed to get her fingers into the eye sockets of two skulls and hoisted herself up just in time.

The two groups chasing her practically collided. They started yelling and arguing over which direction to go. Amy could feel the fingers of one hand slipping out of the eye socket. She maneuvered her hand lower and grasped a mouth opening.

Finally her pursuers agreed on a direction and took off. Amy dropped down and ran the opposite way.

eighteen

I t was light out when Amy emerged from the Catacombs, and she checked her watch. Eight-thirty. With any luck, she'd get back to the hotel before Monica woke up. Just in case luck wasn't with her, she used the time on the Métro to concoct a story that would explain her disappearance.

But she didn't need an excuse. Monica wasn't even there. An excited Madame Anselme handed her a note. Apparently, someone had telephoned the message in English, and this was the hotel manager's attempt to write it down.

La Tour Eiffel. Top. Monica. Kidnap. Alive. Come.

It wasn't hard to decipher the note. Monica had been kidnapped. And if Amy wanted to see her alive, she was to come to the top of the Eiffel Tower.

The hotel phone rang. Madame Anselme picked it up. *"Oui, Madame!"* To Amy she said, *"C'est ta maman!"*

It was Amy's mother calling. For the first time that week, they could talk. Only now Amy didn't dare take up any more time. "Tell her I'll call her back," she yelled to Madame Anselme as she ran out of the hotel. It wasn't until she was back on the Métro that she realized she'd spoken to the woman in English, who probably had no idea what she'd said.

But who had kidnapped Monica? The neo-Nazis? Did they think they could use her to get Amy back? Then another thought hit her. Christophe! He could be holding her for ransom to get money. Anything was possible.

There was a long line of people waiting to board the elevator at the bottom of the Eiffel Tower. Amy jostled through the crowd and ignored the outraged cries as she cut to the very front of the line. She hopped onto the elevator before anyone could stop her. Inside, everyone stared at her with unconcealed hostility. Amy didn't care.

When she finally got off at the top, she looked around wildly for any sign of Monica, or Christophe, or one of the Nazis. But only ordinary tourists were in sight, and the ones who had been on the elevator with her were still giving her the evil eye.

She tried to think. Then in the midst of the oohs and aahs of the crowd admiring the view, a particular voice stood out. It wasn't louder than the other voices—in fact, it was so soft she knew she was the only one there who could hear it. It was Andy's voice.

She stiffened. How low could he stoop? Now he was a kidnapper.

He was calling to her—but from where? She couldn't see him in the crowd. Following the sound of his voice, she moved toward the edge of the enclosed viewing platform.

All of Paris was spread out before her, but now wasn't the time to appreciate the view. Her eyes were fixed on a cast iron railing beyond the protective barriers. Andy stood there, precariously balanced on a bar. Amy was stunned. She couldn't imagine what he was doing there. Even a genetically perfect clone wouldn't be able to survive a fall from the top of the Eiffel Tower.

Then she saw that he wasn't alone. A few yards away, on another bar, stood Sébastien.

Carefully Amy climbed over the barrier that pre-vented the tourists from falling off the tower. Trying not to think about how high she was, she positioned herself on a metal bar between the two guys. Amy spoke first. "So you're one of them too."

Sébastien's voice was even more solemn than usual. "I *was* one of them, I regret to say. But I have seen the error of my ways and have left the group."

"He's lying, Amy." Andy was speaking now. "He's very much a part of the group. He wants to bring you back to them."

"And what do you want, Andy?" Amy asked evenly. "Maybe *you* want to be the one to bring me back, so you can get the credit. I'm surprised Annie isn't out here too."

"I'm not one of them, Amy."

"Oh, Andy, stop lying. I *saw* you wearing an armband. I heard you telling them you'd bring me back."

Sébastien spoke up. "You are correct, Amy. Come to me. I will get both of us down from here safely, and we can go to the police."

"Amy, don't listen to him," Andy said urgently. "You see that helicopter over there?"

There *was* a helicopter hovering above the Eiffel Tower.

"It belongs to the Nazi group. As soon as Sébastien

has his hands on you, that helicopter will come in close enough for him to put you on it."

Amy hesitated.

"He lies, Amy!" Sébastien declared. "You said so yourself. I have summoned that helicopter to rescue us. It has nothing to do with those people in the Catacombs. Andy is the one for you to fear. I have left the group; he remains with them."

"Amy, I'm not with that group," Andy said. "Not now, not ever. I've been spying on them to get information that I can turn over to proper authorities. People who can stop them. I had to pretend to be one of them so I could get their secrets. Sébastien is one of their leaders!"

"That is nonsense! Do I look like a leader?"

Amy had to admit that the guide was no model of physical perfection. She looked at him for a moment. Then she looked back at Andy.

His eyes bored into hers, and she felt that instantaneous connection she'd felt before. But she couldn't trust those instincts anymore. She'd felt that way about Annie, too.

"Come to me, Amy!" Sébastien commanded.

"Amy, please!" Andy cried out. "Come to *me!*"

She was torn; she didn't know what to do. Logic and

emotion were jumbled up together. The question still haunted her: Could anyone be trusted?

Maybe she wasn't as smart as she was supposed to be. Because her heart cried out for Andy. She took a step in his direction.

"Stop!" Sébastien yelled. "I have a gun!"

She froze. She could see the glint of a cold metal weapon in his hand. He was pointing it at Andy.

"Take one more step and I will shoot your boyfriend!"

It must have been her automatic response to the notion of someone harming Andy. In any case, she found herself moving faster than she'd ever known she was capable of moving. She leaped to the next lower rung, swung her legs around, and knocked the gun loose from Sébastien's hand. He reached out to grab it. And in the process, he lost his grip on the rail.

He fell. He fell from the top of the Eiffel Tower. Suddenly crowds of tourists were looking over the barrier, crying out in horror.

For a second Amy couldn't move. Then Andy was by her side. He put his arm around her waist and pulled her back into the tower. There he held her close, and she clung to him just as tightly.

From way below them came the sounds of police horns, ambulance sirens, people screaming. Amy wanted to remain motionless, with Andy's arms around her, always.

But there was still an unanswered question, and an unfinished mission.

"Andy . . ."

"What?"

"Where's Monica?"

nineteen
19

Monica was waiting for them in the fancy restaurant on the second floor of the Eiffel Tower. She was calmly sipping a glass of orange juice as Amy and Andy walked in. Waving at them both cheerfully, she said, "Isn't this place lovely? It was so nice of Andy to organize this brunch. Will Annie be joining us too?"

"No," Amy said, sinking into a chair at the table. "Annie can't make it." Andy sat in the seat next to hers, and under the table he took her hand.

"I've just heard that someone jumped from the top of the Eiffel Tower," Monica went on. "Isn't that awful? Thank goodness no one on the ground was injured."

"Thank goodness," Amy echoed. So Monica had no idea what had been going on. Andy had explained things to Amy on their way down to the restaurant. "I invited Monica to brunch," he'd told her. "And I left that message at your hotel. I knew you'd think Monica had been kidnapped. It was the only way I could get you here. You would never have agreed to see me otherwise."

"Can you blame me?" Amy asked him.

"No. Amy, you'll never know how hard it was for me to pretend to be one of those people."

"But who were you spying for?"

He was silent for a moment. "I was spying for myself. For us. For all the others like us," he said finally. "We have to know who our enemies are, Amy. We have to know their plans."

"We know about the organization," Amy began, but Andy shook his head.

"It goes way beyond that," he told her. "Amy, we have more enemies out there in the world than you or I could ever possibly imagine. We have a lot of work to do, if . . ."

"If what?"

"If we're going to save the world."

She stared at him in disbelief. But by now they

had entered the restaurant and he couldn't say any more.

"You know," Monica was saying, "when I first got Andy's invitation this morning, I thought it might be from Christophe. And Amy, you'll be pleased to know I almost ripped it up and threw it away." She shook her head sadly. "I don't think Christophe was ever really interested in me. I think he just preys on rich women. He was simply using me."

"Oh, I don't think that's true," Amy lied. "He cared about you, Monica. But he wasn't good for you. He was just a—a—" She tried to come up with the right word. Andy supplied it.

"Loser."

For a second he sounded like Annie. But this time Amy agreed with the assessment.

"Hello, everyone!"

Amy turned. "Mom!" She jumped up and hugged her mother. "I'm so happy to see you!"

"Me too," Nancy said. "I tried to call you this morning to ask you about this invitation."

Amy remembered that her mother had never met Andy. Quickly she introduced them. When Nancy heard Andy's full name, her eyebrows went up. She knew the story of Amy's experience at Wilderness Adventure.

"Well! How did you two find each other in Paris?"

"It's a long story, Mom. I'll tell you tomorrow, okay? On the plane going home."

Nancy agreed, and Amy was relieved. She was going to need the time to decide exactly how much she was actually going to reveal to her mother.

They had a lovely reunion brunch. Nancy told them about her conference, and Monica talked about museums. They had just ordered a fancy French pastry for dessert, when Andy stood up.

"Would you please excuse us? I'd like to show Amy the view from the top of the Eiffel Tower."

"Oh, you haven't seen that yet?" Nancy asked. "You must go up there, Amy. It's spectacular."

"Really?" Amy asked weakly and without a whole lot of enthusiasm. But she held on to Andy's hand as they took the elevator back up to the top.

This time they stayed within the barriers, where the other tourists were taking photos. But Andy acted like no one was there except the two of them. He put his arms around her, and he kissed her. Just like in the movie.

It was wonderful. Amy's head was spinning and her heart was beating triple time. It was the most romantic experience she'd ever had.

It was also confusing. Andy still remained a big mystery. Who was he really? What did he want? What was going in his mind and his heart?

Maybe someday she would have the answers. For now she was content knowing that they were on the same side.

epilogue

In the operating room a nurse was assembling the surgical instruments. The surgeon put on his plastic gloves and contemplated the patient lying on the table.

"This is truly astounding," he said to the nurse. "I have never before seen a case where someone survived a fall from the Eiffel Tower."

"He's barely bruised," the nurse remarked. "I am sure he has substantial internal damage."

The anesthetist checked the patient. "He is ready for surgery."

The doctor stood above the patient, scalpel in hand. Suddenly the patient opened his eyes.

"Something's wrong!" the doctor exclaimed. "He's awake!"

"That's impossible," the anesthetist protested.

The patient sat up. His legs moved to the side of the table, and he dropped to the floor. For a moment he just stood there.

"What are you doing?" the nurse cried out. She rushed toward him. The patient thrust out his hand and sent her flying across the room. The doctor and the anesthetist rushed to her side.

"He can't be human!" the nurse moaned.

Sébastien nodded. And he walked out the door.

Be sure to read how Amy first
hooked up with Andy in the
exciting Special Edition

#6
And the Two
Shall Meet

Amy arrives at Wilderness Adventure all pumped up for
a week of extreme sports. Her superior strength gives
her an edge over the others. But she's ready to rock-climb,
mountain-bike, and hang-glide without apologies. Only Eric
and Tasha know why things are so easy for her. And Amy is
glad they've come along—especially Eric, since she's crazy
about him.

But the rugged bonding experience doesn't go exactly as
she's planned.

Amy falls for a mysterious guy. Freak accidents abound. Secrets rule.

Soon "extreme" doesn't begin to describe the mad scram-
ble for survival.

Amy's life will change, all right—change forever!